I0534142

THE LAST REIGN

THE STORY OF THE DOWNFALL OF THE LAST KING OF THE JINN

By Loai Faez Felemban

الناشر

سِيبَوَيْه

سيبويهTM للنشر والتوزيع المحدودة
Sibawayh Publishing
المملكة العربية السعودية – جدة
Jeddah, Saudi Arabia
+966 920004119
info@sibawayhbooks.com

© Loai F. Flemban, 2015
King Fahad National Library Cataloging-in-
Publication Data
Flemban, Loai F
The last reign - Jeddah
ISBN: 978-603-01-7735-6

1- Novels 2- English fiction I-Titel
823.912 dc   1436/3791

He gives power to whom He pleases and endues with honor whom He pleases

Billions of years ago, Earth was ruled by the jinn. They were the masters of Earth, not living in hiding as they are today, but leading a life similar to our present life. They were educated; they worked for their living; they were contented with God's grace and thankful for His favors. However, evil is present in every place and time. In this secret book, which is preserved by them, I specifically chose the last chapter because it narrates the story of King Khorkhis, the last king of the Ashkhor Dynasty, whose reign was characterized by much bloodshed. That was the strongest and most ruthless reign of their time. This chapter marks the time of the founding of the science of witchcraft, sorcery, prediction and the end of their world. How did that defiled work come about? Who established it, and who started using it? And why did it persist till our present day, and how was the formation of the Diabolical Triangle (The Bermuda Triangle) achieved? That is the secret that has puzzled the whole of the human race! Truth is now within your reach, and I shall recount the details in the hope of learning from the jinn's mistakes.

An Illustration of the Branches of the Jinn Dynasty

The jinn were divided into several branches. It is well-known that by God's law, marriage is the basis of creation. Every creature is born from a male and female. So, who are the original father and mother of the jinn?
I shall mention here the father's name only. I withhold the mother's name for personal reasons. He is called Sumia (the First Father of the jinn). Later, they were divided into several branches.

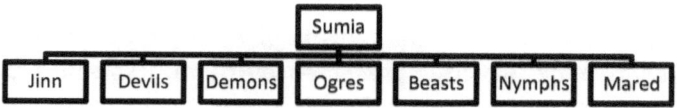

When we mention their names as a group, we call them the Jinn Dynasty…
But they are divided under that name into:

The Jinn: They have numerous forms, some can fly and others are very fast and their strengths differ according to their color.

The Devils: A kind of jinn that do not have many different forms. They cannot fly and they are not known for being fast. They are strong and are characterized by their speedy animals. Some of their animals can fly.

The Demons: One of the strongest of the dynasty. They are outnumbered by the other branches. They are very fast and when they are furious they change their shapes and turn into demons. They become taller and can fly at very high speeds. No one can compete with them.

The Ogres: Jinn known for their strong build. Ogres can endure the harshest circumstances.

The Beasts: Very similar to the Ogres, but their great strength is evident in water. Beasts are amphibians and they cannot dispense with their life in water.

The Nymphs: Well-known for their beauty. They can take several beautiful shapes and some of them can fly. They are similar to the Beasts in that their strength is evident in the water

Merdan (Plural of Mared): They are characterized by leadership and intelligence, as they are very strong and courageous. Of all the jinn, they are the only ones who can compete with the demons.

In the Name of God the Almighty

A very sad day for the empire follows the tragic death of our great King Khafan. The sun sets on our lands and the water canals run dry in our gardens. Let all the roses wither in mourning for you, our great master. The empire will know no other king but you...

This is a public declaration of the designation of King Khorkhis, as King of the Five Devils' Kingdom and the Seven Jinn's Kingdom.

The date today is the Month of the Scorpion, the first day of 1232 Faran.

He possesses the right to be obeyed by all the kingdoms of jinn and devils. He can act as he sees fit for the people, and anyone who receives this parchment shall come and pledge allegiance to King Khorkhis...

Khorkhis: What do you think Bilban? Do you suppose I shall be like my father, King Khafan?
Things are not what they used to be! The rebels are trying to overpower me and pillage all my property.

Bilban: Don't be afraid, master. The rebels are afraid of your army, especially the Black Demonic Army and the Red Jinn Army and of your soldiers, the Flying Jinn. Don't be afraid because we have the six commanders.
1- Commander Sural, Head of the Red Army.
2- Commander Darl, Head of the Princes of the Fire Valley.
3- Commander Fifgel, Head of the Flying Jinn.
4- Commander Torn, Commander of the Seas.
5- Commander Shuja, Head of the Commandos Army.

6- Commander Prince Khaji, Head of the Great Black Army.

Khorkhis: I know that Bilban. However, we have lost three of our greatest commanders, who were holding the Kingdom together.

1- Commander Markhof: Head of the Savage Ogres.
2- Commander Sourfag: Head of the Monsters of the Seas.
3- Commander Mared: King of the Merdan.

Bilban: But master, you know that they had tried to rebel against your father when he was in power, and if it wasn't for Wise Fouta, you could have been in prison now.

Khorkhis: I know that. But those three must be disposed of, because they can defeat most of our commanders.

Bilban: How can you say that, sir? Don't be afraid. Markhof will be confronted by The Black Army and Sourfag will be confronted by Torn, commander of the seas. As for commander Mared, he will give us a hard time and no one can defeat him. We need a tight plan for that purpose.

Khorkhis: We know that Torn cannot confront Sourfag, who is older than him and more experienced in warfare. He also has his supporters, the Beasts, who can destroy the whole of Torn's army. Torn has no sea monsters, his supporters are the nymphs. As for the great Mared, only I can confront him with my own secret army.

Bilban: What do you mean by that, master?

Khorkhis: I want to destroy the three commanders.

Bilban: But sir, there will be chaos and a great war will break out!

Khorkhis: Don't worry, Bilban. We shall catch them unawares. I shall betray them.

Bilban: You're the king, but I have to tell you that a bloody war will break out; one that our world will never forget.

Khorkhis: The war is inevitable. We are not safe from now on and I don't trust anyone anymore; neither the seven kings of the jinn nor the five kings of the devils.

Bilban: Why, master?

Khorkhis: Do you remember the dream that I always used to have and could never explain?

Bilban: Yes, I remember it very well, but I don't think it's that important. Sometimes we dream of things that are on our mind.

Khorkhis: I don't know! Make the preparations for the celebration and the reception ceremonies. The kings of the jinn and devils will be here any minute.

(This statement might sound strange and the story might seem ambiguous; but this is what happened millions of years ago. At that era, those were the masters of Earth before mankind, and they were divided into Merdan, ogres, jinn, devils and nymphs. The ruling family, then, were the descendants of the Ashkhor Royal Dynasty. The last king to rule from that family was King Khorkhis. He was young of age and was considered the first king to be in power at such an early age. King Khafan and all his brothers and older sons had been struck, one after the other, by a strange fatal disease; all except Khorkhis. Some thought that Khorkhis had done that to his family to seize his father's throne. He was reputed for his recklessness and foolhardiness and was a person who believed in dreams and visions; a fact that helped him a lot during his reign when he had tried to mend what his forefathers and ancestors had built; a hatred of their family by all the kingdoms. Khorkhis wanted to make reforms, but sometimes one wishes upon something and the contrary happens. Those are the events that destroyed their world and made them what they are today).

The Forbidden Zone

That zone did not recognize the reign of King Khorkhis' family. All the rebels inhabited it. Anyone who was exiled from the kingdoms of jinn and devils went there. Everyone knew that it was a time bomb. King Khorkhis and his predecessors had kept it under their tight grip and planted spies and traps to prevent its inhabitants from causing chaos in their world. It was ruled jointly by the three exiled leaders: Markhof, Sourfag and Mared, together with their great army. It was named, The Three Kingdoms. Anarchy was dominant in that zone. Murder, vice, adultery, kidnapping and rape were prevalent. No law governed that zone. It was the survival of the fittest, and the three leaders and their supporters were the fittest.

Shurar: Master Mared, I have received some news that you should be aware of.

Mared: What is it, Shurar? You know I'm not in a good mood today and I'll kill you if I don't like what you have come to tell me.

Shurar: King Khafan is dead.

Mared: What are you saying, Shurar? Are you sure this news is true?

Shurar: Yes, I received this news from the Kingdom of the Five Devils. A parchment was delivered to each king to pledge his allegiance, and it was read in all the public squares. I have brought you the text of the speech.

Mared: Read it to me Shurar.

Shurar: In the name of God the Almighty

A very sad day for the empire follows the tragic death of our great King Khafan. The sun sets on our lands and the water canals run dry in our gardens. Let all the roses wither in mourning for you, our great master. The empire will know no other king but you...

This is a public declaration of the designation of King Khorkhis, as King of the Five Devils' Kingdom and the Seven Jinn's Kingdom.

The date today is the Month of the Scorpion, the first day of 1232 Faran.

He possesses the right to be obeyed by all the kingdoms of the jinn and devils. He can act as he sees fit for the people, and anyone who receives this parchment shall come and pledge allegiance to King Khorkhis...

Mared: Finally! Khafan is dead!

May the earth worms devour you and the fires of the sky burn you. The journey which I have planned to embark on starts today. Shurar, summon commanders Markhof and Sourfag. We shall pay the miserable King Khorkhis a short visit.

Markhof and Sourfag: What is it Mared? What made you send for us during our time of leisure?

Mared: Brothers and dear friends, I want to tell you something that will make you very happy.

Markhof: What is it Mared? Is it another penalty?

Mared: No Markhof, this time we shall impose the penalty!

Sourfag: What are you hinting at, Mared? We are too drunk to reflect upon your riddles right now.

Mared: It won't take long. Shame on you! You are the commanders of ogres and sea monsters. Is that the appearance of a leader? Where is your pride?

Sourfag: Don't forget our value, Mared, and stop mocking us.

Mared: Very well, brothers, the news that I bear to you is...he's dead, at last, King Khafan died after a reign that lasted 400 years.

Markhof and Sourfag: Is that possible! Khafan, the king

11

Mared: Yes, finally, thank God. I thought he would still age further and outlive us. Do you know what that means?

Markhof: Do not persist with your riddles, Mared.

Mared: Khorkhis has announced the news to all the kings of the jinn and devils. They are all going to his palace to swear allegiance and loyalty to the new king. So, we shall also join them and congratulate him on his new reign.

Sourfag: Have you gone mad, Mared? You know that he has forbidden us from leaving this land or else we shall die.

Mared: Who's going to kill us? Answer me. Have you forgotten that we are the strongest in the empire?! Even Khafan was afraid of us when he sent us into exile.

Markhof: Very well, how do you want us to leave this land when we are so tightly guarded?

Mared: Get ready. We shall get out on our own. We can do that now, because we are allowed to leave without our armies.

Sourfag: Good… Let's go then.

The Gate of the Forbidden City

Guard: Hey, you three. Stop and identify yourselves.

Mared: Are you scorning us, you stupid guard?

Guard: Forgive me, Master Mared. I didn't recognize you, but you know Khafan's instructions.

Mared: Khafan is dead. Our agreement stated that we could go out but without our armies.

Guard: You have been here for 300 years and you never went out. Why do you want to do so now knowing that your blood will be shed if you leave without the king's permission? I know the constitution very well. If you want to go out now, you should get the permission of King Khorkhis.

Mared: Then tell your king that we have come to congratulate him on his new reign, which is not going to last.

Guard: Mared, do not step out of line.

Mared: Can you kill me then? You know I could slaughter you right now.

Guard: You know that the traps that had been laid for you and your people can kill you. Even if you kill me now, the king will know and he will exterminate you all.

Markhof: Who's going to exterminate us, the new inexperienced king? ... Ha ha.

Guard: King Khorkhis is still a new king, but his six commanders will destroy you.

Sourfag: So, let it be.

Sourfag couldn't control himself. He threatened to kill the guard if he did not let them get out of the Forbidden City, even if a war would break out.

Guard: I shall send for King Khorkhis now, wait.

13

Sourfag: Have you gone mad? You make commanders like us wait?
Mared: Sourfag, let's calm down. You will get everything I promised you, and we shall realize all our dreams.

The Empire of Ashkhor

Messenger: Chamberlain Bilban!

Bilban: What do you want? Why are you here? Isn't it your duty to guard the gate of the Forbidden City?

Messenger: Yes sir, but something dubious is happening.

Bilban: Speak, guard. What is it? The look on your face implies there's a tragedy.

Messenger: Master, the three commanders Mared, Sourfag and Markhof are standing outside the gate requesting permission to pass.

Bilban: What? Is that possible? And what do they want?

Messenger: They say they want to congratulate King Khorkhis on his new reign.

Bilban: Could that be possible!

King Khorkhis: What is all this commotion? Is anything wrong Bilban? And why are you here guard? Isn't it your duty to guard the gate of the Forbidden City?

Bilban: Sir, someone is requesting your permission to enter.

King Khorkhis: And who is that?

Bilban: The three commanders.

Khorkhis: Who? Is that possible!

Bilban: Master, they are waiting at the gate of the Forbidden City. What do you want us to do?

Khorkhis: This is an obvious challenge to my powers; they are belittling me. So be it. Guard, go tell them that the king welcomes them.

Bilban: Master, there will be the seven kings of the jinn and the five kings of the devils and the six commanders. They will look upon you as a traitor to your father's reign

15

for giving permission to these three commanders to leave the Forbidden City and offer their loyalty to you.

Khorkhis: I am the king, and my followers should have trust in me.

Bilban: Master, I don't know what to say right now. I feel that something unexpected is going to happen.

Khorkhis: Bilban, where is Wise Fouta?

Bilban: He's gone on a journey of repose and God's worship.

Khorkhis: I wish he were here. He could have guessed their intentions now and helped me in making the right decision.

Bilban: Master, I'll stay with you, no matter what happens.

Khorkhis: Take this parchment and read it to them.

The Forbidden Zone

Messenger: Guard, let them pass and here is the stamp of permission.

Guard: What are you saying? Is it possible that he has given them permission?

Messenger: Don't worry. King Khorkhis is challenging them.

Guard: Mared, the response has come.

Mared: Finally! I'm bored with waiting.

Guard: Mared, I shall read out to you now my master, the king's parchment:

In the name of God the Almighty

He gives power to whom He pleases and endues with honor whom He pleases...

I thank God that he has made me king to serve His Kingdom and rule the land with honesty and justice. It came to my knowledge that you wish to pay me a visit and bless my new reign and era.

I do not object to your wishes. May God bless your moves and curse your bad intentions if it should be your wish to destroy our land. This letter is a pact between me and you, pledging your safety while you are on my land, as long as you extend your hand in peace, and God is my witness.

Eternal peace or total destruction

King Khorkhis

Mared: We agree to the conditions of the great king.

Guard: Then bring your stamp to conclude the pact.

The three commanders: Here is our stamp for the king's parchment.

Guard: Then you are welcome to pass through in safety.

Mared: Now brothers, do not try to do anything foolish in front of King Khorkhis. Let each one of you offer him his allegiance and obedience.

Sourfag: Very well Mared. It's going to be a hard journey as we haven't visited the empire for the last 300 years.

Markhof: Mared, what if Khorkhis tries to betray us? We do not have our armies to confront him.

Mared: Don't be afraid. King Khorkhis cannot do anything. The text of his letter is a pledge. I have left a note to my servant, Shurar, that if we do not return in ten days' time, he should get the rebels ready, bring the soldiers and besiege the empire.

Markhof: What about the army at the gate? How can they penetrate it? The fort, as you have seen when we were going out, is very tightly guarded.

Sourfag: Yes. Have you seen the flying jinn? There are also the ogres that I used to command and the Black Demonic Army as well as the concealed death traps.

Markhof: What a mean and cunning king he was, King Khafan! How shrewd he was! Tell us Mared, how can this barrier be penetrated if we do not return in ten days?

Mared: Don't rush things. Brothers, there is time for everything and you will know everything. I am preparing a plan and I don't want anything to distract me.

Sourfag: We are approaching the gates of the empire. Get your permission stamps ready.

In the Empire of Ashkhor

18

Bilban: My master King Khorkhis, the ceremonies have been prepared and the kings are on their way to you.

Khorkhis: Bilban, I have given it much thought. How about assassinating the three commanders while they are here, in the presence of all the kings of the jinn and devils?

Bilban: Master, this is an unwise decision and conduct. These are the ceremonies of your investiture as king and emperor of this country. Is that how the beginning should be? The kings and commanders will suppose that you are an unwise king and that you have broken your pact.

Khorkhis: I am their king and I know the interests of this country more than they ever will.

Bilban: Because of this knowledge, you think of betrayal? Master, do you want to begin your reign with assassination? This is a bad omen. Moreover, there is your pledge in the text of the parchment, how can you break it?

Khorkhis: Since when do we care about omens? I believe in what I do, and God willing, He will bless my move in purging the earth of them. As for the pledge, you are aware, Bilban, that war itself is deception.

Bilban: Sir, do not do this in the presence of the kings. Even the three commanders are not easy to get rid of. I think that Mared has prepared an alternative plan for this visit. I swear to you that this visit is his idea and you know that he is a wise decision maker. Your father used him to conquer the harshest countries that no one could ever conquer. The Valley of Fire, that had been the graveyard of the Ashkhor Dynasty and their army, was defeated only by Mared and he was able to impose their obedience and loyalty to your father. He also forced them to pay an annual ransom. Do you suppose he is going to let you murder him now? I don't think so at all!

Khorkhis: What's wrong with you Bilban? Are you scared? You told me you would be on my side no matter what the circumstances were.

Bilban: Yes master. I'm with you till death. However, since I am your chamberlain and minister, I advise you to reconsider your decision before executing it.

The messenger from the empire gate: My master, King Khorkhis.

King Khorkhis: What do you want?

Messenger: Sir, the first guests to pay allegiance have arrived.

Khorkhis: Then let them in. What are you waiting for? Who are the first arrivals, the kings of the jinn or the kings of the devils?

Messenger: Sir, the three commanders are awaiting your permission to enter the palace.

Khorkhis: What? Is it possible that they have arrived so soon?

Bilban: Didn't I tell you, sir? Beware of them; they are well-known for their speed. Take care, master.

Khorkhis: Bilban, bring in the six commanders right now. Let the reception be as grand as I want it to be.

Bilban: Yes sir. They are coming right now.

Guard at the gate: Commanders, are you familiar with the royal instructions regarding receiving the guests who are coming to pledge allegiance and obedience?

Mared: It's a wonder how things have changed here! Look Markhof, weren't the statues of the victories that I offered to King Khafan placed over here? Where did they go?

Markhof: Perhaps the new king doesn't like anything with our names on it.

Sourfag: And look how the empire has changed! It wasn't like this when we were exiled.

Guard: Commanders, I'm not going to repeat my question, please listen.

Mared: You damned child, I swear if you had been in the Forbidden City I would have made you food for my animals.

20

Guard: Mared, you are now in King Khorkhis' city. Don't force me to make you food for the emperor's animals, you traitor.

Sourfag: What are you saying, you wicked man. By God, I shall kill you now.

Mared: Calm down, Sourfag. The day will come when we shall find this guard and teach him a lesson he'll never forget. What is your name, guard? Or are you afraid to tell us?

Guard: I'm only afraid of God who created me. My name is Charle.

Mared: Very well, Charle. We haven't finished our talk yet.

Emperor's messenger: Charle, read them the instructions for entry.

The guard, Charle:

In the name of God the Almighty

This is the code of loyalty and obedience of every great king or commander or prince who wants to pay allegiance to King Khorkhis and avoid his anger. Peace be upon you all…

Keep your heads down as you enter, and let your eyes look downward until the king gives you permission to look up. You must bow and straighten up until he gives you his blessing to kiss his hands and forehead. Then, you shall take your designated seats. Do not ask many questions as this is the Inauguration Day.

King Khorkhis

The guard Charle: Commanders, seal it now if you want to pledge allegiance.

Markhof: Mared, Sourfag, do you accept his conditions? They are a challenge to us.

Sourfag: By God no! This is meant as an insult to show us how unimportant our positions are to him and that he doesn't care for us. Since when is this code recited? We are familiar with it. In the past, we were the ones who read out the entry declarations.

Mared laughed disrespectfully.

Markhof: Is this the time for disrespect, Mared?

Mared: This indicates that the king is afraid of us and that he wants to affirm his royal identity. He is provoking us with this message so that we commit a foolish act and provide him with an excuse to kill us.

Markhof: How did you know that?

Mared: Look above, Markhof, at the surveillance rooms. Do you see anyone there?

Markhof: No, there's no one.

Mared: And you, Sourfag, look. How many guards are there at the gate?

Sourfag: There are only ten guards.

Mared: Is it possible that Khorkhis does not protect himself and his kingdom when he knows that we are coming?

Markhof and Sourfag: Then what does Khorkhis have in mind?

Mared: His soldiers were right behind us when we reached the borders of the kingdom. We all know that the soldiers who guard the gates are the most skilled soldiers; they are the heads of the city. Have you noticed how the guard, Charle, was addressing us in a provocative manner? They want to infuriate us to have an alibi to kill us. Look behind you, Markhof, and you, Sourfag, you will see some soldiers disguised as common people and peddlers. Since when there are peddlers in this area! I swear to God these are soldiers. Look up at the sky. You will see the flying jinn hovering above us at far distances thinking that I would not take notice of them. I can smell the six commanders watching us now and expecting us to make a single mistake. I shall pretend that I'm quarreling with you and you will see the reaction of those who pretend they are peddlers. If they are really so, they will ignore us. If not, then you'll see them react. Shortly after, commander Mared pretended that he was quarreling with Markhof and that he was going to kill him. What Mared had said about the common people and the peddlers was true. They were all watching them as if they were on the alert.

Sourfag: You are right, Mared. They are soldiers.

Markhof: How clever you are, Mared. How did you know that?

Mared: Didn't I tell you to trust me? I shall be the ruler soon. Come on, get up before the guard, Charle, suspects us.

Charle: What is going on, commanders? Has your stay in the Forbidden City made you lose your minds?

Mared: Excuse us, Charle. We haven't come upon an advanced civilization such as yours yet.

Charle: Spare us your mockery and stamp your consent now.

Mared: At your command, Charle.

Charle: Now, the messenger will guide you to the location and may God be with you.

After the commanders had stamped their approval, they went to the location of the ceremony. Their minds were filled with ideas and plans, but they felt afraid as well. Markhof and Sourfag did not know what Mared was thinking of, but they did trust him.

At that same moment, King Khorkhis was disconcerted. He was hoping that his plan would work out.

Bilban: Master, the six commanders are here.

23

Khorkhis: Let them in quickly. I want to hear the news.

Bilban: What news?

Khorkhis: You will know soon.

Bilban: I hope it is good news. Great commanders, you are most welcome to enter in peace.

Commander Khaji: My master, King Khorkhis, they only just escaped our trap!

Khorkhis: What happened, Khaji, prince of my great Black Devils Army?

Khaji: I don't know. But the guard, Charle, tried to provoke them and he succeeded in doing so. What followed was what we had thought would happen; Sourfag and Markhof lost their nerve and we got close to attacking them, but Mared calmed them down.

Khorkhis: Woe to him! What else happened?

Torn: Sir, I think Mared is aware of our plan.

Khorkhis: Why do you say that?

Torn: Because I saw Mared whispering in Sourfag's ear.

Khorkhis: I don't suppose it was something important. He might have been giving him instructions only.

Fifgel: No, sir. I don't think so. The winds transmitted some of their whispers to me. I was with my army of flying jinn and I heard some of their words. Mared said it was a trap.

Khorkhis: Are you sure that you have heard right, Fifgel?

Fifgel: You know, master, that I'm the commander of the flying jinn. God has favored me with powerful sight and hearing.

Darl: Master, I was one of the princes of the Valley of Fire before we joined your blessed reign. I was also the commander of one of the armies there when your father ordered dominance over the Valley of Fire. You know very well that the soldiers of the Valley of Fire are the most ruthless fighters. Despite that, Mared was able to

24

topple us and overpower us. He was so quick-witted and very clever in taking decisions.

Khorkhis: Commander Sural, what's wrong with you? Why aren't you taking part in this conversation?

Sural: I don't know what to say to you, sir.

Khorkhis: Speak, Sural. You are the commander of the Great Red Army. What's wrong?

Sural: Sir, I don't want to give you such news now, but I'm going to speak. You should be informed.

Khorkhis: Speak up, Sural. By God, you have made me lose my nerves now!

Sural: Sir, the spies of the Red Army told me about an attempt to overthrow you.

Khorkhis: Who dares to do that?

Sural: It's one of the five kings of the devils. But I don't know his name yet.

Khorkhis: How did you know that? How can you relay insufficient information to me?

Sural: I didn't want to talk about it until I was sure of its truth. But as today is the day of the pledging of allegiance, you must be informed.

Bilban: What's all that, master? Where do I stand in all this? Why didn't you tell me what you were doing?

Khorkhis: I wanted it to be confidential. I don't want to discuss this subject.

Bilban: But, sir, I'm your chamberlain and I was your father, King Khafan's counselor. He entrusted you to me and asked me to remain by your side so that you do not do anything that could harm you or your reign.

Khorkhis: Bilban, please listen to me now. I must come up with an alternative plan soon.

Bilban could not believe what was happening. For a moment, he suspected that Khorkhis did not trust him anymore. Bilban did not like that feeling at all. He felt belittled and underestimated. He had been the counselor of the royal court ever since Khafan became the crown prince. How could Khorkhis do that to him!

The emperor's messenger: My master, Khorkhis, will you give your permission to the three commanders to enter now and pledge their allegiance? They are waiting outside the ceremony chamber.

Khorkhis: Come, my commanders, and stand beside me. Let them see who I am and how great my power is. Bilban, show them in.

Bilban: At your command, my master, the king.

The emperor's messenger: Bilban, here is the parchment of the agreement to the conditions of the allegiance, stamped by the three commanders.

Bilban: If they agree to the conditions, then I don't know what you are going to do, Khorkhis. But, by God, you will regret it. *You were right Khafan when you told me prior to your death that your son's decisions are rash.*

Bilban looked sad and discontented with the recklessness of King Khorkhis. He knew that his decisions would increase the number of his enemies and cause his downfall. But there was nothing he could do. He was only the king's counselor and his chamberlain. A young king like Khorkhis would not listen to him and would only do what he wanted to do.

Bilban: Lasting peace. Welcome to the empire of King Khorkhis. Long live the king.

Mared: Hello, Bilban. You have become an old man now! What has life done to you, cousin?

Bilban: Mared, you are aware that our kinship should remain a secret and that you chose to be a traitor.

Mared: My dear Bilban, I swear to God, if you were not my cousin, I would have killed you along with the soldiers who took me to my exile.

26

Bilban: Mared, have you listened to the royal instructions regarding receiving the guests and understood them very well?

Mared: Yes, chamberlain.

Bilban: Let's go. The king is waiting for you.

King Khorkhis wanted to appear in all his glory because, deep down inside, he was terrified of Mared who had been his teacher when he was a little boy. He had trained him to fight and he had also coached him on the administration of armies and the tactics of war and planning. That was an important meeting for both of them. That's why Khorkhis wanted to impress Mared and show him that he did not fear him even though Mared had been his teacher.

Bilban: My great master, King Khorkhis, I submit to you, and in the presence of the six brave and strong commanders, the allegiance of the Forbidden City represented by its three commanders: Commander Mared, king of Merdan, commander Markhof, commander of the savage ogres and commander Sourfag, commander of the sea beasts. They have come from their exile to offer you their good intentions and to remedy what they had spoilt during your father, Khafan's, reign. May a new page begin in your era and may the past be forgiven. This is the parchment of the allegiance stamped by them.

Khorkhis: Welcome to my great kingdom. Did you see any changes?

Sourfag: Yes, we have seen things that we did not have during your father's reign.

Mared: Hello my dear pupil. I see you have become a king now. However, I can still detect some of the foolhardiness of childhood in you.

Khorkhis: How are you, Markhof? And how are your ogres? Are they still hungry as I remember them; always eating?

Markhof: Yes, that's right. And every day they grow bigger and stronger than before. They could now break iron with their teeth if you let them!

Mared: Didn't I tell you that you are still a foolhardy child? Are you ignoring me and trying to provoke me? Wasn't your attempt to betray us and violate the pact enough for you?

Khorkhis: And you, Sourfag, how many sea beasts do you have? Torn here says that his nymphs can defeat your beasts.

Sourfag: I 'm not in the mood for laughter now. Mared is asking you a question, and you didn't answer him!

Mared: Leave him, Sourfag. He's my pupil and I know how to conduct myself with him.

Khorkhis: Are you threatening me, Mared?

Mared: By God, no! How can I threaten a great king like you?

The emperor's messenger: With the praise of God, the seven kings of the jinn and the five kings of the devils have arrived.

Sural: Master, please do not try to provoke them now. One of these kings is trying to kill you. If he sees the three commanders and realizes that you are trying to provoke them, he will join forces with them. The kings of the jinn and devils have brought their armies.

Khorkhis: Damn you, Mared. You're still the same. The years of exile had no effect on you and your strength. Bilban, let's receive the kings now.

Mared: How wonderful! The kings are here. It's going to be a fantastic ceremony.

Khorkhis: You are still under oath, Mared. Your stamp is witness to that. So, be polite.

When the kings of the jinn and devils entered, they were startled to see the exiled commanders. Each one of them was thinking to himself whether it was possible that King Khorkhis had forgiven them so quickly and easily. All eyes were on them. The kings went in to kiss the king's hand and brow and offer their pledge of loyalty and obedience. When Mared approached to kiss the king's hand, Khorkhis refused.

Mared: Why don't you let me kiss your hand? Are you afraid?

Commander Khaji: Mared, hold your tongue. If the king doesn't want your greeting, just stay away.

Mared: As you wish, Khaji, commander of the Black Devils.

Sourfag: Markhof, why is Mared behaving in this manner? Why is he humiliating himself?

Markhof: Believe me, Sourfag. Mared has a big plan. You know Mared doesn't accept an insult.

Bilban: My master, King Khorkhis, these are the parchments of the covenant presented by the seven kings of the jinn and the five kings of the devils and stamped by them.

Khorkhis: Bless you all for your loyalty to me. May God bless you in your life and your reign. As my father used to say to me, unity is what protects the nation from those who want to shed blood and destroy the country. By God, with our unity, we shall become a powerful hammer that will break our enemies' necks. I shall be like my father, even greater. Peace will prevail during my years of sovereignty. And God will help me.

Sural whispers in Khaji's ear: I hope what he says is true. I swear I can see blood flooding the valleys.

Khaji: What's wrong with you, Sural? Don't you trust your king?

Sural: Later on, I want to tell you something that the six of us should know.

Khaji: So, be quiet now. The secret soldiers are everywhere.

Khorkhis: And to prove to you that I'm right, and that I want to make the coming years peaceful ones, I have just forgiven the three commanders and I'm making them kings of the Forbidden City, but under guard, until they prove their efficiency.

Everyone was surprised at the king's decision. How could he forgive those who attempted to assassinate his father? Over and above, news from the Forbidden City always reached him and he knew that they were tyrants. He should have killed them instead of forgiving them!

Khorkhis: Dinner is ready, if you please. When you finish, you can leave in peace. Bless you all for the allegiance. History will record this day and the nation will attest to your peace and righteousness.

All the guests proceeded to have dinner. Mared and his companions refused to stay and apologized for being unable to stay on the pretext that they could not leave their city without any ruler. The king gave them permission to leave. As soon as dinner was finished, the kings of the jinn and devils excused themselves too and went safely on their way.

The Kingdom of the Five Devils

This kingdom was considered more powerful than the kingdom of the jinn because the devils were higher in rank than the jinn. Before the Ashkhor Dynasty reunited the country, they were always at war. Devils were stronger in build, but the jinn surpassed them in education and armament. Thus they used their brains to defeat the devils. The country was governed by five rulers, who governed the five states that were reunited by King Khafan. Before that, they resembled the Forbidden City. There was still some chaos and disobedience of the law. That was why Khafan chose, from among them, a great leader. It was Khaji, the commander of the ruthless Black Devils Army.

The names of the five kings of the devils were:

1- King Rakhel
2- King Sharaeel
3- King Zaiboun
4- King Anafeer
5- King Asater

Those were the five kings of the devils. They were the fiercest kings, all reputed for their might and cruelty. It was the duty of anyone who wanted to become king of the devils to kill a thousand people, burn them, drink their blood and eat their flesh. The kings of devils had to be very rough due to the harsh environmental conditions they lived in. The eldest and most dominant among them was King Sharaeel.

King Rakhel: What did you think of the allegiance ceremony today?

King Zaiboun: I don't know. I think I saw distrust in the eyes of the six commanders.

King Asater: I say he will not be like his great father Khafan.

King Zaiboun: Did you notice how sure Mared was of himself? By God, he has something on his mind. How could Khorkhis accept their allegiance? His father was extremely cautious of them. It is well known that Mared is cunning and sly.

King Anafeer: Brothers, I see it differently.

The four kings: What do you think, Anafeer?

King Anafeer: I think Khorkhis is very frightened. And because of this great fear, he's making rash decisions. Do you remember when we pledged allegiance to his father, Khafan? He was alone, without the six commanders. As for Khorkhis, he had them stand on his right and left. It was as if he wanted to show us how self-confident and proud he was. Also, allowing the three exiled commanders to pledge allegiance for him, and then refusing to be greeted and kissed by Mared, because he was afraid that Mared would kill him, was an irrational act. If you are king, fear not. Be confident, especially with someone like Mared whose era knew no assassinations. In all his wars, he resorted to confrontation.

King Rakhel: Do not forget, Anafeer, that Khorkhis is still too young. He wasn't supposed to be the crown prince. Were it not for his brother's death of that disease and all his other brothers afterwards, he would still be a young prince now.

King Zaiboun: But isn't it strange that all ten brothers died and Khorkhis was the only one who stayed alive?

King Sharaeel: I swear to God that I have suspicions about their deaths. Is it plausible that they all died of the same disease, even Khafan, but nothing happened to Khorkhis? How could that be?

King Asater: Why do you say that, Sharaeel? I'm sure there is something you want to say.

King Sharaeel: Yes, there's something I'd like to say, but we must make a pact here and now that if Khorkhis' reign is overthrown, we will remain united so that we don't perish too.

King Zaiboun: What are you saying, you crazy man? Who can overthrow Khorkhis' reign? The six commanders can destroy any king.

King Sharaeel: Brothers, we all wanted to revolt against Khafan, but we were afraid of being exterminated. But today, something strange happened to me.

The four kings: What happened, Sharaeel?

King Sharaeel: Mared was looking at me as if he wanted to tell me something. His look was dubious. Do you remember when he excused himself and did not have dinner? As he was leaving, he passed by my side and put something in my cache. I was afraid that one of the six commanders or secret guards might have noticed. I tried to remain composed. When we arrived here, I opened the letter and read it. By God, it's a very serious letter.

King Rakhel: What did Mared write to you?

King Sharaeel:

In the name of God the Almighty,

O great King Sharaeel, peace be upon those who follow the light of the sky...

I want to tell all of you five kings that I am going to overthrow King Khorkhis' reign. So either you will assist me or stay out of my way when I attack him. We have been patient for so long and we all know that King

Khorkhis, the weak reckless boy, is not fit for this position.

If you are not on my side, then you are against me. If you're with me, you will be safe from my fury. If you're against me, you will meet the same terrible defeat as that of Khorkhis.

God is witness to my words, and peace be upon those who follow the light of the sky.

King Anafeer: My God! Why is Mared threatening us this way? Is he so sure of himself?

King Rakhel: You heard the content of the letter. What are you going to do now? It seems that Mared is sure of what he's doing.

King Zaiboun: Couldn't this be a scheme of Khorkhis' to test our loyalty to him?

King Asater: No, I don't think so. Khorkhis doesn't have enough experience to come up with such schemes.

King Sharaeel: So, brothers, what is our position now?

King Asater: Was this letter delivered to the kings of the jinn, or only to us?

King Sharaeel: I don't know. But the kings of the jinn are very loyal to Khorkhis' family. I don't think this letter will have any influence on them. They will inform Khorkhis of it.

King Rakhel: I don't suppose that Mared would forget them. The jinn are very clever and their knowledge surpasses our strength. So I don't think Mared forgot them.

King Anafeer: If the seven kings of the jinn stand by Khorkhis, we can never overthrow him even if we unite with Mared.

King Rakhel: So, Anafeer, do you want to overthrow Khorkhis?

King Anafeer: Yes, I do. Till when shall we keep on kissing the hands and heads of the Ashkhor Royal family? We want to be our own masters; no one should dominate us!

King Zaiboun: I agree with you on that.

King Asater: But you are aware that kissing him is not just out of loyalty. It is for the sake of protecting ourselves from anyone or any army that tries to attack us.

King Rakhel: We don't want his protection. We have enough armies to safeguard ourselves and our lands.

King Sharaeel: So, brothers, whose side are you going to take?

King Anafeer: But we have pledged allegiance to King Khorkhis, and we have stamped it. You know what breaking a pledge means and its consequences.

King Asater: Yes, we know. That's why it's going to be a difficult decision to take.

King Sharaeel: And what if we break the pledge? Laws were made to be violated.

King Zaiboun: Have you gone mad, Sharaeel? By God, if we break the pledge and were defeated, our heads will be cut off. Do not forget the six commanders. Have you forgotten the Black and the Red armies? Our army cannot hold out against them. Remember also the flying soldiers and the army of nymphs. Khorkhis is still very powerful. How will Mared be able to leave the Forbidden City when he is kept under guard from all sides, and the traps that could exterminate his whole army are everywhere? How can he get out? Even if we pull out our guards from the Forbidden City, the guards of the jinn will stay there and Khorkhis will suspect us and send his armies to get us. He is reckless and cannot be argued with.

King Rakhel: You are right, Zaiboun. Why didn't I think of that! I'll tell you what the solution is. How about being in the middle? We remain loyal to Khorkhis, and if we see that Mared was able to leave the Forbidden City with Markhof and Sourfag, we take their side. But if we see Mared and his friends fall in the traps and not many of them survive, then we fight them and take Khorkhis' side.

King Asater: I think we should take Khorkhis' side. He's still the strongest.

King Rakhel: No, Asater. You don't know Mared very well. By God, he will do what he wants to do. That's why we should gain his favor.

King Sharaeel: So, if Mared's messenger comes, I shall give him the parchment. Give me your stamps to seal the agreement.

The five devils agreed to Mared's plan on condition that they switch sides as they see fit; to support the victorious and kill the defeated. However, deep down inside, they were all terrified as that was going to be the first coup in the history of the Ashkhor family.

The Kingdom of the Seven Jinn

This kingdom was one of the most advanced in sciences. They were superior to other kingdoms in their architectural and urban development, as well as their armament. They were very peaceful, but in times of war, they discarded their peace clothes and wore their war clothes. King Khafan's father, who was called King Sharmaoun, ordered his son to marry one of their girls in order to make peace with them. He knew that war between them would only bring death to both parties. Khafan married the daughter of King Rah, whose name was Sanaheb. She was very beautiful and she bore him a son, Khorkhis. Thus the connection between the kingdom of the jinn and the Ashkhor family became very strong. It wasn't just a peace treaty, but also a blood relationship. Their rulers were very loyal to the kingdom. Of their soldiers who served under King Khorkhis' command then, were Commander Torn, commander of the nymphs and apostles, and commander Sural, commander of the Red Army and commander Fifgel, commander of the flying jinn.

The names of the seven kings and queens were:

1-Queen Sunial (Queen Tuyour): Queen of the flying jinn.

2- Queen Rukhah (Queen Houran): Queen of the nymphs.

3- King Shamoun (King Saleh): King of the good jinn.

4- King Ouran (King Ahmar): King of the red jinn.

5- King Seeran (King Aswad): King of the black jinn.

6- King Dwan (King Katel): King of the fighting jinn.

7- Queen Niran (Queen Sheikha): Leader of the kings of jinn.

Queen Sheikha: Kings and queens, today we have kissed the head of a new ruler and the youngest son of the Ashkhor family, King Khorkhis. But, my God, he's still so young! Do you remember when we congratulated Khafan on the day of his son's birth?

Now he's the king of the strongest country and kingdom of the Ashkhor family. We have to support him as he is the son of our princess, Princess Sanaheb.

Queen Tuyour: Then we suggest the marriage of Khorkhis to one of our princesses in order to renew the pact that we had made.

King Katel: I suggest we marry him to one of the daughters of our commanders; like Torn's or Sural's or Fifgel's daughter. This way, they will renew their loyalty to him and defend him for fear of shame. Thus the defense will be stronger.

King Saleh: I suggest we not only marry him to a princess of the jinn, but also to a princess of the devils to strengthen the ties.

Queen Houran: We know that the devils will refuse this request. They are loyal to him to gain his protection and because of the strength of his army.

King Ahmar: But how could Khorkhis act like he did today! We are all for peace but not with Mared and his friends because they still bear a grudge against Khafan.

King Aswad: Yes, this is an indication of his young age and his lack of wisdom.

Queen Niran: Enough with this talk. Chamberlain Bilban and Wise Fouta are always by his side to help him in his decision making.

King Katel: We are passing through difficult times. The peaceful era that lasted twenty thousand years has gone.

Situations have changed even in our kingdoms. There are lots of murders. So we must take matters firmly in hand before they get worse.

Queen Houran: I'm going to change the subject slightly. Today, my nymph told me something that I would like to share with you. I had sent her on a journey across the seas and oceans to bring me news of the jinn and devils in remote and exiled lands. She told me something that I could not believe.

Queen Sheikha: Something about the cursed zone? Yes, I did hear about it from one the flying soldiers. I didn't give it much thought because I wasn't convinced of what he told me. Go on, and let's hear what you have to say.

Queen Houran: But my nymph told me that after she had crossed some distance inside the cursed city, she had the impression that no one inhabited it. Then she saw a child devil walking and then suddenly disappearing out of sight. She got very scared. She said that the small devil was dressed as a slave, meaning that he belonged to someone who lived there. What shocked me more was his disappearance. How could that happen? My nymph was so scared that she didn't have the courage to follow him. When she wanted to turn back, she heard strange sounds and saw sea beasts, the likes of which she had never seen before. The strangest of all was that they attacked her with no regard to her mission and her costume which indicated that she was one of us. The nymph killed them and escaped.

Queen Sheikha: What you're saying is very serious, Houran. Are you sure of it?

Queen Houran: Yes, you can also ask my nymph.

King Saleh: I have heard about that zone and its legends. But I don't think they are true. I suppose your nymph was very tired after her journey.

King Katel: I don't think they are true either. However, if they are, then why haven't we heard anything about them?

King Ahmar: It's not in the nymph's interest to lie. Sunial, you own the fastest flying jinn. Let them go over there. Perhaps they will detect something.

King Aswad: My concern is that it could be a secret place for the rebels. I shall send some of the black jinn with them.

Queen Sheikha: Do what you think is right, but I hope this information is untrue. Messenger, bring us one of the flying jinn and another of the black jinn. Choose two who possess strong intuition and great speed.

The messenger: Very well, your majesty.

The messenger headed to the military zone and met with the commanders of the armies. He informed them that the queen wanted one of the flying jinn and one of the black jinn who were known for their speed and cunning. When the commanders asked him why, he said: "I don't know. The queen wants them immediately, without delay". So the commanders chose two of the most skilled jinn soldiers: the flying jinn, Harek, and the black jinn, Sahek.

Messenger: Your majesty, Queen Niran, the commanders send you their greetings and they have dispatched the soldiers that you requested: the flying jinn, Harek, and the black jinn, Sahek.

Queen Sheikha: Bless you, soldiers, and may God bless your footsteps. I shall read out your mission now.

In the name of God the Almighty,

Peace be upon the soldiers of God and glory to his prophets...

Soldiers, we have received a report from the nymph who had gone on a peace mission. There is a country beyond the six seas that you know, called the cursed zone. It is uninhabited. She reported that she saw a small devil in a slave's dress but he disappeared the moment she laid eyes on him. There were also mutinous sea beasts that attacked her with no regard to Thus, they have violated the peace treaty, signed below, on the fifth day of the Gemini, in the year 3248, Faran. Hence, we are cleared of this treaty. Kill whoever attacks you and imprison everyone you can take as prisoner, but use your intuition because we suspect the presence of rebels and outlaws there. I have chosen you specifically because of your skills and I hope you will not disappoint me and betray my trust in you. God is on your side. Fly in peace. Sahek, we shall send with you the black bird to fly you as well as the fast birds of peace to bring us back the news. We shall also send the nymph to show you where the incident took place. God bless you.

Sahek and Harek: We hear and obey, your majesty. At your service.

Sahek and Harek flew up in the sky, with great speed, toward the six seas, until they arrived to their destination.

Nymph: Stop here. This is the area where I saw the child devil.

Harek: Is that possible? This is the cursed zone. Is there anybody here? I can only see the fog.

Sahek: And where did the sea beast attack you?

Nymph: Right here. But the strange thing is that he did it after the disappearance of the child.

Sahek: If you had killed the beast, then where is his body now?

Nymph: I don't know. This is strange. I killed him here.

Harek: Maybe the other beasts devoured him. It seems to me that this is a savage place.

41

Sahek: Bird, put me down right here. I want to wander around and explore this place.

Harek: I'm going down with you. If you see anything suspicious, nymph, go back to the seven kings and inform them about it. Don't wait for us; we can take care of ourselves. We shall enter the city and walk around for two hours; then we'll come back to you.

Nymph: No, I'll stay here with you. This is also my mission. I'll stay here and protect you from harm. Fly away, dove of peace and tell the queen about what's happening here.

Sahek: My God, what's this foul smell emanating from this place?

Harek: Beware, Sahek. I have heard strange legends about this place.

Sahek: What have you heard?

Harek: I have heard that there is a hidden cursed city here which pursues its own desires, and doesn't believe in prophets and disobeys God in return for supernatural things.

Sahek: What supernatural things?

Harek: They say there's a person here, whose sect I do not know, who might be one of the merdan or the devils or the jinn or the ogres. He's called Saher.

Sahek: Yes. I've heard that. I've also heard that Saher asks you for things, and in return, gives you whatever you want. But I don't think this is true. Where is he? He hasn't appeared either in war or in peace.

Harek: Some say he caused the death of the Royal Ashkhor Family from a strange disease that no medicine could cure.

Sahek: If what you say is true, then why didn't he kill Khorkhis too?

Harek: I don't know. That's what has been rumored lately.

Sahek: A hidden city? Could it be possible? This resembles the bedtime stories that we tell our children. Haven't you noticed something queer about the nymph, Harek?

Harek: Such as what?

Sahek: Her ambiguous story. Devils don't disappear. How can she say that?

Harek: Keep in mind that this is the cursed city. Her tale could be true because if the city is cursed, then its inhabitants should stay out of sight. However, it's her story about the sea beast that I did not believe.

Sahek: And why?

Harek: First of all, the sea beasts do not come to this area because of its high salinity level. Beasts cannot live in this high concentration of salinity.

Sahek: Do you think the nymph is lying?

Harek: I'm suspicious of her. My intuition tells me she's plotting against us.

Sahek: What shall we do now?

Harek: Listen to me. We shall interrupt this search mission. The nymph is waiting for us. We told her that we were going to wander about for two hours. It's only been half an hour. We shall secretly fly up and watch her to see what she's up to.

Sahek: But she will take notice of us. Nymphs have an intense sensation.

Harek: I know. But we too are very fast. Throw your weapon here and blow it. She will turn toward the source of the sound. Just at that moment, I'll take you high up from the other side so that she won't be able to spot us.

Sahek: All right, then.

43

Harek and Sahek executed their scheme and reached the highest sky. They both had very strong eyesight. They went very high up, away from the nymph's sphere of vision.

Harek: At this altitude, it's difficult for the nymphs to see or hear us.

Sahek: Let's watch her now.

Harek: Sahek, it's been one hour now and she hasn't moved yet. Do you think we have been unfair to her?

Sahek: Let's wait until the appointed time has passed. My intuition tells me she's hiding something. I suspect that she brought us here for a reason.

An hour and a half later, something unexpected happened.

Harek: Look at the nymph, Sahek. She is making strange movements as if she's gesturing and calling out.

Sahek: Oh my God! Look at her. She has killed the birds of peace and the black bird!

Harek: What do you think? Shall we attack her or go and tell the kings first?

Sahek: No, let's wait. No matter how strong she is, she cannot defeat us. Look over there, some people are coming. Who are they?

Harek: How terrible! This is the uniform of Mared's soldiers! Aren't they supposed to be in the Forbidden City?

Sahek: Do you think they want to trick us?

Harek: There are only fifteen minutes left till the end of our mission. Let's keep an eye on them. They are hiding behind the rocks. How many of them do you see?

Sahek: I see only two.

Harek: Then the plan is the following: I shall take you down there, and you have to move quickly so that the nymph doesn't see you. You blow the trumpet to signal

44

our return. She will get ready. I shall handle the other two. I shall kill one of them and take the other as prisoner.

Sahek: And the nymph, what shall we do with her?

Harek: We want to keep her alive to stand a fair trial. Sahek, go ahead and exchange your peace insignia with the war insignia.

Harek brought Sahek down to the cursed land, and they moved with a speed greater than the speed of lightning. Sahek blew the return trumpet, and the nymph and her companions prepared themselves to kill Sahek and

In a few seconds, Sahek attacked from the front and Harek from the back with supreme force. Harek killed the first soldier and held the other one prisoner. Sahek captured the disloyal nymph and they proceeded with great speed to the kingdom of the seven jinn. Minutes later, they arrived to the palace and stormed in without permission.

Queen Sheikha: Why did you break into the palace with such force? And why did you capture the nymph? Who is that person with you?

King Saleh: My God! Have you exchanged your peace insignias with war insignias?

Queen Sheikha: What happened? Tell us.

Harek: Your majesty, we have accomplished our mission according to your orders. However, Sahek and I suspected something weird in the nymph's words. We suspected her and our suspicion was right.

Queen Sheikha: What are you saying? Tell me what happened.

Sahek: Your majesty, the story that the nymph had told you was only sheer fantasy. There was no devil in the Cursed City and no sea beast that tried to kill her either. The zone that the nymph pointed out to us is uninhabited. It is impossible to live in it because of the high level of salinity of the sea. We drew up a plan and went very high upward. From there, we witnessed an unexpected act. We saw the nymph killing the birds of peace and the black bird. She wanted to kill us with the help of this man and another soldier. We took them by surprise; we were able to kill the other soldier and took her and this man as prisoners.

Queen Sheikha: Is what they are saying about you true, nymph?

Nymph: I have nothing to say. Kill me.

All the kings of the jinn were shocked. They denounced her act. They had so many questions to ask. How and why? Who ordered her to do that? The nymphs were renowned for their fierce loyalty and utmost obedience to the kings. Every time one of the kings questioned her, she would only say: "Kill me. Don't ask too many questions. I'm bored with your foolish questions." That nymph was the head of the maids-in-waiting of Queen Houran. Thus it was a big shock to them.

Queen Houran: How could you betray me, my own maid-in-waiting?

Nymph: You fools, who claim to be kings and queens! I'm only one of them and you were able to expose me. But there are many more like me.

Queen Sheikha: What do you mean by many? Whom are you referring to?

Nymph: As far as I know, you are not stupid, Sheikha. I shall die now, but there are many others. You will be betrayed and you will all die.

Queen Sheikha: Chamberlain, prepare the justice square and let everyone come and witness her punishment so that she would be an example to other traitors.

Kind Aswad: Well done and bless you, Sahek and Harek. But who is that? Do we know his identity?

Sahek: I don't know. He doesn't speak, but his costume indicates that he's one of Mared's soldiers.

Kind Aswad: Mared! Could this be one of his soldiers? His soldiers are in the Forbidden City. Soldier, is it true that you are one of Mared's soldiers? Why don't you speak? I'm talking to you.

Sahek: Sir, let's kill them all and inform King Khorkhis about it.

Queen Sheikha: That's right—because he's not going to talk. Kill them all now. Prepare the justice square now and let all the soldiers and commanders attend.

In those times, that was the first execution of a maid-in-waiting who served one of the kings of the jinn. The nymph was Queen Houran's favorite maid. Everybody felt the tragedy. Even the commanders and their soldiers were shocked by the nymph's actions. They all wondered why she had done that. Each one told a different tale about the reason for her punishment. They all gathered in lines and the seven kings arrived. The judge came and started reading the statement:

In the name of God the Almighty -

"God is the king of heavens and earth, and God is the light of the sky. We all are his faithful servants. We rule by His religion and we never disobey Him and worship no other but Him. In the name of God we start, and with prayer for the prophets we conclude. On this day, the month of Pisces, the fifth day of the year 1232 Faran, The nymph—the maid-in-waiting of the great Queen Houran—was sentenced to be executed for overstepping her position as a nymph, and daring to lie and trying to assassinate the two soldiers, Sahek and Harek, while on a mission to the Cursed City. She disrespected the code

47

of peace and endeavored to bring disorder to the kingdom of peace and among the seven kings of jinn. She was sentenced to be punished together with those who assisted her. And whoever will assist her shall get a severe punishment. God is witness to my words. There will be no mercy. Even if the traitor turns out to be one of the senior commanders, he shall receive the death penalty. And with a just punishment, I end my speech.

We conclude in justice and in God we believe. Judgment and praise to you O God; you are just and it's only You we obey. Prayer for all the prophets."

After finishing his speech, he closed the book that had too much dust on it. There hadn't been an act of treason for thousands of years, ever since the epoch of the great wars, which was long before the founding of the Ashkhor dynasty. The law stated that the traitor should be executed by his king or queen. That meant that Queen Houran was the one who should execute the nymph. It wasn't going to be easy for her. Houran was soft-hearted and she sympathized with the nymph and loved her very much. The term maid-in-waiting signified that she was her minister and advisor on all matters as well as her chamberlain. How difficult this situation was, in addition to the experience that she had to go through. The kings of the jinn knew the law very well. There were certain ceremonies for that execution in order for it to be an exhortation and a lesson to others. It should be carried out with a sword that wasn't very sharp so that the convicted person would bleed and die slowly.

And while the person was dying, the executor would take some of that blood to wash his face with. He would thus be denouncing that sinful blood. That was the law that had been practiced since the era of their ancestors. They could never change it.

Queen Sheikha: Houran, you are familiar with this law. Can you implement it?

Queen Houran: I shall implement it and I shall not weaken. I don't want anyone to say that I'm a weak queen. But, by God, it's a situation that I shall never forget.

Queen Sheikha: You realize that this is for the welfare of the nation. You are not being unjust to the nymph. She has brought this on herself.

Queen Houran: So, let me get on with it. Judge, bring me the sword of justice now.

The judge: At your command, my queen. Here is the sword of justice; the sword that we judges pass on from one generation to another. The last punishment was executed with this sword one thousand years ago. We shall inscribe today's date and the nymph's name on it. The name of the person executed by this sword should be written on it.

Queen Houran: My God! Are all these names inscribed here the names of traitors?

The judge: Yes, your majesty. If you please, and we do felicitate you on your action, take this parchment and read it out to your maid-in-waiting.

Queen Houran: What is this parchment?

The judge: This is the parchment of the seal of dishonor. After the nymph answers the questions written in this parchment and her neck is cut off and your face is wiped with her blood, you take the parchment and wipe your face with it so that the seal of dishonor is imprinted with the nymph's blood and you are purged from her.

Queen Houran: Good, let's go to her now, judge.

The judge: In the name of God, we begin.

Houran went to the execution square, wearing the insignia of fury, which signified the gravity and

49

seriousness of the situation. It also meant that whoever was wearing it had no mercy in his heart.

Houran stood in front of the nymph and all the commanders, soldiers and kings. She said out loud, "Shame on traitors." She opened the parchment and started the questioning. That was the procedure of trials in the jinn's world. The king posed the questions and the convicted person answered.

Queen Houran: Do you confess to the charges made against you?

Nymph: Yes, and I want to be punished.

Queen Houran: Do you realize that you have betrayed your religion and your country?

Nymph: Yes, and I'm prepared to bear the consequences.

Everyone was surprised by the nymph's courage. Anyone standing in that square would be scared, unable to speak, and would beg for forgiveness. But the nymph was so courageous that some thought she must have been sick. Others said that she wasn't a nymph. Something weird was going on!

Queen Houran: What happened to you, my nymph? Answer me!

Nymph: I told you I want to die.

Queen Houran: Why did you do it?

Nymph: What's wrong with you, Houran? Has your heart softened?

Queen Houran: Are you mocking me? Damn you. No more questions. Die without mercy.

The queen raised the sword and brought it down on the nymph's neck, but only halfway through. She did not continue because she wanted her to suffer while she was dying. The nymph's blood scattered in all directions, while Houran stood proudly and put her foot firmly on the nymph's head and said: "Die in suffering, not in peace."

The commanders and soldiers were fearful of Houran's terrible appearance. She said: "God damn every traitor, God damn every traitor." After the nymph's death, she executed the unknown soldier too. When she finished, she did what the law stated. She washed her face with the blood and wiped it with the seal of dishonor parchment. She said: "Do not bury her. Cut off her body and crucify it on the gate of the city." Later on, the judge took the sword and said: "Well done, my great queen. With this, we close the page of treason."

Queen Sheikha: Well done, Houran. Now change the insignia of fury with that of peace.

Queen Houran: No. I shall not remove it as long as there are traitors.

Queen Sheikha: And who would dare try after this?

Queen Houran: Have you forgotten what the nymph said? I must check it out.

Queen Sheikha: As you wish. Judge, send your messenger to King Khorkhis to tell him what happened.

The Forbidden Zone

Markhof: What's wrong with you, Mared? You haven't been all right ever since we came back. Is something wrong?

Mared: No. By God, I'm thinking about a very serious matter.

Sourfag: What is it, Mared?

Mared: When we were on our way out, I put a short message in the cache of one of the kings of devils.

Markhof: Which one?

Mared: It was King Sharaeel.

Sourfag: Are you crazy Mared! King Sharaeel! You know that the great Black Devils Army is one of his armies. He had offered this army as a gift to King Khafan. He's one of Khafan's supporters.

Mared: Yes, and that's why I did it. I know that Sharaeel relinquished his army in return for peace to his country. He's waiting for the right opportunity to get his army back.

Markhof: If you are so sure of your intuition, then why are you so tense?

Mared: Because we shall leave the Forbidden City now.

Sourfag: Leave! How can we leave?

Markhof: Mared, How can we leave when Khafan surrounded us with guards and traps that could kill us?

Mared: Have you heard of the Cursed City?

Markhof and Sourfag: Who hasn't heard of it and its incredible legends and fictional stories! Everybody talks about it.

Mared: And you must have heard about a person called Saher and his two friends, Habel and Nabel?

Markhof: Yes. But of course these people do not exist!

Sourfag: Mared, are you saying that you believe the legends about Saher and Habel and Nabel?

Mared: I swear these people are real and they will get us out of here.

Sourfag: Do you mean that they can make you disappear and take you anywhere you want? Since when can we disappear!

Mared: Sourfag and Markhof, I shall tell you a secret that I have kept to myself for a long time.

Markhof: What is your secret, Mared?

Mared: I shall tell you about the great battle of the Valley of Fire and the secret of my disappearance there.

The Great Battle of the Valley of Fire

The Valley of Fire was a region inhabited by all sorts of jinn and devils and ogres and merdan. It was not specified for any one sort. In ancient times, it was called the Valley of Rivers but the name was later changed due to its proximity to the Cursed City, which was then called the Green City because of the abundance of trees and greenery in it. After Saher's curse on the Green City, the rivers were ablaze and they have been burning ever since. It was rumored that the Green City was cursed by an unknown person called Saher. He was the cause of destruction of the Green City, as the legend went. The city's militants were extremely tough. The ogres were well known for their strength, and the devils for their cunning, and the jinn for their speed, and the merdan for their leadership. How could anyone overpower such an army! It was a danger to the Ashkhor Royal Family. Many a king of this family had tried to exterminate them but they were always defeated. It was the only region that used to launch attacks on the kingdom at various times until Khafan, Khorkhis' father, became king. At the time, Mared was the commander of the royal brigades, while Markhof and Sourfag were among the six commanders.

Mared's story

King Khafan: Mared, we have received some unpleasant news.

Mared: What is it, sir?

54

King Khafan: I have heard that the armies of the Valley of Fire are going to invade the nearby lands. If they succeed, then we lose the trust of the seven kings of the jinn and the five kings of the devils. What shall we do? You know how hard my forefathers tried to overcome them but to no avail. They are extremely strong and numerous.

Mared: Leave them to me, sir. I shall take care of this matter.

King Khafan: Mareo, you know that you are my best commander. I can't afford to lose you. Are you sure you can defeat them?

Mared: I shall defeat them. Just give me the authority to form the army that I want.

King Khafan: Your request is granted. And here's my seal; use it the way you want. But Mared, you know what the law states when a king gives his seal to one of his commanders.

Mared: I shall go now and prepare the army that will win us victory over the princes of the Valley of Fire and their soldiers. Don't worry, I know the law very well and I won't betray you.

Mared left, feeling very confident. The king had put his trust in him and had given him his seal. That meant that the king had placed his hopes in him. If Mared was defeated, it meant his death because he would have brought shame to the king. Shame is washed away with the defeated commander's blood. That was why Mared tried to be very cautious. He was reputed for his intelligence and shrewdness. While Mared was getting his army ready, Wise Fouta was with the king, giving him his blessing for the impending war.

Wise Fouta: Is Mared one of the commanders that you trust?

King Khafan: I don't know, Fouta. I'm in a very difficult position and I had to take this decision.

Wise Fouta: Giving your seal to Mared might lead to a revolt against you. This seal is the king's seal and now he is at liberty to do what he wants and his orders should be obeyed, even if the price was your life.

King Khafan: I know the law. But if I ignore the princes of the Valley of Fire, they will eliminate the cities of the jinn and devils and I shall be considered unworthy of their allegiance. How could that be when we collect protection taxes from them!

Wise Fouta: I think that Mared will be victorious.

King Khafan: I do hope so. That's why I have made him commander of my brigades!

Wise Fouta: May Mared win this war for us and bring you the victory that you deserve.

The Military Zone of King Khafan's Army

Mared: Commanders, I have come here to tell you that I shall invade the region of the Valley of Fire. Here is the king's seal that gives me the authority to choose the army that I want. Anyone who hears his name called out will come forward now. Commander Sural, commander of the Red Army, commander Fifgel, commander of the flying jinn, commander Khaji, commander of the great Black Devils Army, commander Sourfag, commander of the sea beasts and commander Markhof, commander of the ogres.

The five commanders: Ready to hear your orders, Mared.

Mared: I don't want the whole army. Just choose ten of your most skilled soldiers.

The five commanders: Mared, Have you gone mad? Do you want to conquer the Valley of Fire with fifty warriors only?

Mared: Not fifty but sixty. Don't forget my soldiers. This is not about the number of soldiers. How many times have we tried to conquer them only to be defeated? Follow my plan and do what you are ordered to do.

The five commanders: All right, Mared. We are at your service.

The five commanders did their best to classify and select their most skilled soldiers. For that specific battle, they needed war experts with very strong builds. After they finished the selection process, they brought Mared fifty warriors.

The five commanders: Your orders have been executed, Mared. What's the plan now?

Mared: According to our spies, the princes of the Valley of Fire are preparing an army to break into the city of the jinn and devils. However, we know that the kingdom of the jinn and devils is surrounded by very strong walls. It will be difficult for them to break into it, but they will try anyway. My guess is that they only want to cause confusion and affirm their presence and shake the kingdom. The princes of the Valley of Fire will proceed to the kingdom of the jinn and devils divided into two armies.

One army will be dispatched to the jinn and the other to the devils. They will think that we are going to confront them with all our armies. You will be in the forefront, standing at the city walls. You will also be divided into two groups. The first group—Sourfag, Markhof, and Fifgel—will be at the jinn's wall, and the other group—Khaji and Sural—will be at the devils' wall. Their zone will be left without a strong army to defend it.

The five commanders: And how can we penetrate the city when its walls are so strong?

Mared: We shall do it with the help of the sea beasts. I chose only sixty warriors so that they don't take notice of our moves. We are only few in number but we are strong. The sea beasts of Sourfag are known for their resistance to fire. So they will be our means of entry. The sea beasts will float in the river of fire - wearing the uniform of the soldiers of the Valley of Fire - and they will emerge from the main estuary of the river of fire which leads to the east entrance gate. Afterwards, the flying soldiers of Fifgel will fly in the sky, dressed as common people, to distract the guards' attention. Thereupon, the sea beasts will kill the soldiers at the east gate. The soldiers at the other gates will not be alerted because the east gate does not overlook the other gates. It is set apart from them.

While still dressed as common people, we enter through the east gate after it is opened to us. The ten sea beasts complete their mission by quietly killing all the guards at the other gates. There are five gates that we should firmly control. I - along with the ten merdan and ten devils - will proceed to the palace and kill their ruler, King Shirah, - capture his chamberlain- as well as Darl, his commander. Then we purposefully allow two of the flying guards of the palace to escape -in order to inform their army- so as to scare and disperse them. That's when they will come back to try and dominate the city. We close the gates and besiege them and you will be right behind them. We attack them from both sides so that they lose control. I shall later come and throw King Shirah's head in the battlefield. Their king's death would scare them and they would surrender. But we shall not have mercy on them or take them as prisoners. We shall cleanse the earth with their pools of blood.

The five commanders: It's a good plan but full of risks.

Mared: Yes, I know that. But if we firmly implement it, we shall certainly win. I am very confident of my plan but you have to follow the instructions and never violate them. Whoever violates them will be cut to pieces and crucified. Is that understood?

The five commanders and the soldiers: At your command, Mared.

Mared: Let's move now! The Valley of Fire army is already on its way to us.

Mared and the sixty soldiers headed towards the region of the Valley of Fire. Everyone, with the exception of Mared, was scared. They all knew that region well. It was called the graveyard of the Ashkhor Royal Family. The last battle took place between King Shirah and King Sharmaoun, King Khafan's father. Although King Sharmaoun's army was one the most powerful and ruthless armies; it was nevertheless defeated. Sharmaoun was about to lose his whole army so he surrendered. Shirah persisted with attacking the fences until the Devils Army arrived and stopped him. Thus Shirah withdrew and turned back. That battle could have put an end to the kingdom, had the devils not interfered. And now Mared wanted to seize the region with sixty fighters only. That was sheer madness.

Mared arrived at the estuaries of the rivers of the Valley of Fire and they started putting the plan into action.

Mared: Come now, soldiers of the sea beasts, proceed with our blessing. We shall be waiting for you at the east gate. Do not slow down. I want you to move as fast as you can.

Mared and the soldiers headed to the east gate concealing themselves behind the rocks, waiting for the gate to be opened. The plan depended on liberating the east gate. They waited, very tense, until they received a signal. The sea beasts succeeded in killing the guards and opening the gate.

They entered hurriedly and closed the gate. They headed to the city. Mared ordered the sea beasts to complete their mission. He ordered the Red Army to accompany the sea beasts to stand guard at the gates after killing the guards. He also ordered the Devils Army to join him and the merdan to break into the palace of King Shirah. Thereafter, the flying jinn flew high up making an exhibition of fantastic gestures to attract attention. The merdan and devils were known for their extraordinary speed, and they soon arrived to the palace where they were stopped by the guards.

Guard: Who are you? What do you want?

Mared: We want to see King Shirah.

Guard: Why do you want to see him?

Mared: We want to tell him a few things concerning King Khafan.

Guard: Wait for a while. The chamberlain will be here soon.

Mared: Listen, soldiers. We shall break into the palace right now. My guess is that there is no one in the palace except the guards and some soldiers. There are no snipers on the palace minarets. This means that they have gone with the army to attack the kingdom. Get ready. The guard has gone and there's only one left. Let's kill him and storm the palace. I want you to attack with your utmost power.

Guard: Chamberlain, some people want to see King Shirah.

Chamberlain: Who are they and why do they want to see him?

Guard: I don't know. They didn't identify themselves. They just said that they wanted to tell him a few things concerning King Khafan.

Chamberlain: This is strange! What do they look like?

Guard: They are devils and merdan.

Chamberlain: Merdan and devils! My God, what do they want? I shall go and inform Commander Darl. Guard, go to Commander Darl and tell him to come quick. Who might they be?

Guard: Yes, sir.

The guard went to see Darl and on his way, he saw blood on the ground. He was confused, and then he saw that Mared and his soldiers had broken into the palace.

61

Mared caught the guard and asked him, "Where is King Shirah?"

Guard: Who are you?

Mared: I'm Commander Mared, one of King Khafan's commanders.

Guard: Then our army was defeated, is that possible!

Mared: Not yet, but it will soon be defeated.

Guard: I refuse to tell you where the king is and Commander Darl is coming to get you.

Mared: Commander Darl! I've heard about him but he's not stronger than me.

Mared's soldiers: Commander, we have found Shirah.

Mared: Then I don't need you anymore. I'll kill you now. Mared killed the guard and stormed into the king's bedroom. He found him lying in bed, looking very old and sick. The chamberlain was beside his bed.

King Shirah: Who are you? Are you mad! How can you break into my room in this manner?

Mared: Hello, great king! I have always wanted to meet you. My God how old you have become, Shirah! Hello chamberlain.

King Shirah: You are Mared! My God, how did you come in here?

Mared: It's good to know that you have recognized me. So, you are not senile yet.

King Shirah: How could I forget you! You murdered my son during the great wars.

Mared: And now I'm going to murder the father too.

Darl: Stay in your place, Mared, or I'll kill you.

Mared: Welcome, Darl. I see you have come alone. Where is your army? Have they gone to meet their end yet?

Darl: Stay away from the king or I'll cut your head off.

Mared: I want to take you prisoner. By God, I need you to take my place as commander after me. What do you think? You are now in my grip and you know that I can kill you. You either surrender or we fight and you know that you're not as good a fighter as I am.

Darl was silent for a while. In the first place, he wasn't of great importance in the Valley of Fire. Darl was one of the jinn princes, but he was among those who were unjustly exiled. He was a good commander. Were it not for the revolts against him during the great wars, he would now have become one of the seven kings of the jinn. Darl thought about it and said to himself, *Mared is much stronger than me and he would kill me if I stood against him. He has ten devils and ten merdan with him. I have no chance with them. Mared was able to break into the palace with twenty soldiers only. My God, Mared, how did you do it! How did you come in through the gates! Is it possible that he seized the city! Such a commander can destroy the whole army of the Valley of Fire while I stand here with my hands tied, torn between the greed and avarice of the princes of the Valley of Fire. By God, no! I shall not be on your side, Shirah. You are a tyrant, unlike Khafon. I shall determine my fate now and do the right thing as I always have.*

Darl: Mared, I'm on your side. But will you make me commander?

Mared: You'll have what you want, Darl. To be honest with you, I shall let you lead my ten devil soldiers immediately. But you will obey my orders. Do you agree, Darl?

Darl: I'm at your service, Mared.

Mared: Now cut off King Shirah's head.

King Shirah: What are you doing, Darl? Are you crazy! It is because of me that you stayed alive, and now you want to cut my head off. I should have killed you.

Darl: The reason for my staying alive was God's will, and only God will make me kill you, you tyrant.

Darl took the sword and stood over King Shirah's head. He decapitated him without mercy. Then he did the same with the chamberlain. Mared realized that Darl would become someone of great significance. His wisdom would get him what he wanted.

Darl decapitated King Shirah and said to Mared: "Do I stand in good stead with you?" And Mared said: "You do indeed. Now as I have promised you, listen carefully. The army of the Valley of Fire will be arriving. Two of the palace guards have fled, with my knowledge, to deliver the news of the attack on the Valley of Fire. The imperial army will follow them in a hurry after they receive the news. We shall be in front of them. We assault them and you go out pretending that you're wounded. You will be the secret soldier who will spread the rumors among the soldiers to scare them. You will tell them that behind these walls there is an army of black devils and merdan who have assaulted the palace and wreaked havoc on the city. They will be frightened. I shall throw King Shirah's head in the battlefield, after the trumpets are blown, so that everybody can see it. You will cry out loud: 'King Shirah is dead! What shall we do! The king is dead!' The army will be confounded and disorganized. After that you will go to see the princes of the Valley of Fire. Protect yourself with your shield as soon as you see the arrows flying toward them. Kill each one of them with the arrow that I will give you now. This arrow is poisoned. The poison is so fatal that it would kill the person with just one stab.

There are four princes and here are ten arrows. Try to accomplish this deed without letting them take notice of you. You stab one after the other while our arrows are falling on them, so that they think it's one of the flying arrows. Do you understand your mission, Darl?"

Darl: Yes, Mared. I do. When are the soldiers coming?

Mared: Any minute now. The guards who have escaped are on their way to them now. I can feel their scared hearts beating.

The news reached the armies of the Valley of Fire princes. After their siege of the kingdom of jinn and devils, they themselves were now besieged. They announced their withdrawal, which was what Mared wanted, and retreated hurriedly. At that time, they were surprised by King Khafan's commanders.

At the wall of the jinn

Fifgel: Could you have done it Mared? If you did, I'll testify to your cunning.

Sourfag: Let's catch up with them as Mared ordered.

Markhof: Soldiers, move quickly in their pursuit.

At the wall of the devils

Khaji: My God, Mared has done it. Come on, Sural. Let's catch up with them.

Sural: Soldiers, move now.

The armies of the princes of the Valley of Fire arrived to the borders. The flying jinn went to Mared and told him: "The army is here now. Let's get ready." Mared took the head of King Shirah with him and asked Darl: "Are you ready now, Darl?"

Darl: Yes, I am. Let's go and defeat their army.

Mared: Go out quickly through the gate and throw yourself on the ground so they can see you. Go.

Darl: At your command.

The devils and the merdan: Mared, don't you think he has done all that to escape and then betray us?

Mared: No, I don't think so because he was persecuted here. You don't know who Darl is! He is the son of the king of jinn, Shaem. At that time, the jinn kingdom was ruled by one king only. That was before the situations deteriorated during the great wars. He is of royal origin and he keeps his promise. Don't worry. If he betrays us, he will die in the siege. Darl is too clever to betray because he knows what awaits him if he remains on our side. Come on, let's go to the city wall. The miserable army has just arrived.

Mared and his companions headed to the wall. The Valley of Fire army was in a state of shock as they watched the walls of their city with their gates closed. They did not know what had happened. Mared appeared then and said: "Peace be upon those who follow the religion of God. I stand in front of you as a judge who will sentence you and execute his sentence. You have wreaked havoc and shed a lot of blood. You have murdered innocent people and authorized the murder of everyone who had a peace pact with you. You have spread fear and terror among harmless people. From where I stand I tell you that destructive burning is your only ally. You are caught between me and our army. What will you do now?

The merdan then blew the trumpets and Mared raised King Shirah's head up in front of the soldiers and their commanders. They were shocked and could not believe what they saw. Mared threw the head into the battlefield, and Darl did as he was told and succeeded in spreading rumors and scaring the warriors. Mared and the imperial army started throwing arrows at them from all directions, like pouring rain. Darl hid behind his shield and started stabbing the commanding princes, one after the other, all the while shouting: "The commanding prince died!" Hence the army lost its strong pillars. They dropped the flags and surrendered. Darl was picked up by one of the flying jinn and Mared initiated a mass murder.

Mared wanted to kill them all, sparing no one. The gates of the Valley of Fire were opened and the sixty warriors set about killing hundreds of soldiers. It was a severe bloody battle for the army of the Valley of Fire. Some of the soldiers tried to escape but Mared followed them by himself and threw his poisoned arrows at them until he killed them all except one who was carrying a parchment. He wanted to know where he was going and to whom he wanted to deliver the parchment. That soldier entered the Cursed City. Mared was surprised and said to himself, *where is that madman going, no one lives there!* Mared followed him until the thick fog hid the soldier out of sight. Mared looked right and left but he did not know which way to go. He could not see anything. There was very thick fog in the Cursed City and it was said that whoever entered it never came out safe. Mared started moving around in an effort to get out of that labyrinth. Then he saw two persons clad in weird clothes. He shouted at them: "Who are you? Identify yourselves or else I shall kill you."

Smiling, they answered him: "Calm down, great Commander Mared. We are the assistants of our master, Saher. My name is Habel and this is my brother, Nabel.

Mared: What Habel and Nabel! And you say you are the assistants of your master, Saher? This is a myth. No one by the name of Saher exists and neither do Habel and Nabel. This is a superstition.

Habel and Nabel: Are we a myth too?

Mared said to himself, *my God, this is strange! They look the same as they were depicted in the drawings. Is that possible?*

Habel and Nabel: What brought you to our world, Mared, and what do you want?

Mared: I was fighting a battle against the Valley of Fire.

Habel and Nabel: True. And you won a great victory.

Mared: How did you know that?

Habel and Nabel: Saher had told us that before you invaded them.

Mared: What are you saying? This is blasphemy. I swear to God that I'll kill you!

Mared was not able to move. It was as if something was clutching his feet. He was amazed and said to himself, *my God, what's wrong with my foot! It is not moving. What's happening to me! He tried to move but it was useless.*

Habel and Nabel: Stop Mared or you'll break your foot. Our master, Saher, is coming to see you now.

Mared: What have you done to my feet, you fools? I shall kill you as soon as I get rid of this strange feeling.

Saher: Fire to my supporters and peace to my enemies. How was the battle, Mared? You have won a great victory.

Mared: Who are you? What kind of a greeting is that! Uncover your face.

Saher: I shall not reveal my face, but I shall introduce myself. My name is Saher.

Mared: What! Saher! So you do exist and you're not a myth. Is it true what they say about you, that you perform supernatural things, and that you had cursed this Green City and caused its destruction?

Saher: You know so much about me. Then why do you ask so many questions? I don't appreciate that.

Mared: Damn you, Saher. What have you done to my feet?

Saher: This is one of the supernatural things that you have heard about. Your foot is not moving, do you know why? It is because four strong devils are holding it tightly. They are invisible and you will never see them. This is part of the extraordinary things that I do.

Mared: What are you saying? How can our people disappear? Are you mad!

Saher: I shall reveal them to you now to see for yourself. Saher started saying strange, unintelligible words and making incomprehensible gestures with his assistants. Then he suddenly said, "Show yourselves now, my devils!" The devils showed up in a split second and held Mared's foot. Mared was startled by that sight and exclaimed: "My God, how could you do that?"

Saher: I'm going to let you in on a little secret. Mared, you will be exiled to the Forbidden City with two other commanders. After that, you will become a great king.

Mared: Only God knows these things, Saher. Are you an infidel?

Saher: You will know everything later. This is an amulet that you can use when the time is right. Habel and Nabel will be there for you.

Mared: I don't need you or your assistants, Saher. Do you understand? Who's going to send me into exile with two other commanders, when I am Mared, leader of the great merdan and Khafan's advisor! Who dares to do that?

Saher: Enough with your interrogations! I don't like too many questions. I shall imprint this amulet in the palm of your hand. You will need me when the time comes.

Mared: What time?

Saher: When you decide to leave your exile.

Mared: You are still saying exile, you fool! I'll come back for you, Saher, and take you as prisoner to King Khafan.

Saher: It is Khafan who will be sending you into exile.

Mared: Who? Khafan? That's impossible.

Saher: You will see with your own eyes what's going to happen. Now, you will faint and when you wake up you will find yourself on the thresholds of Khafan's kingdom. Do you know how many days you've been here, Mared?

Mared: Days! It's only been a few hours.

Saher: You have been here for a week. Our time is different from yours, and my time is up now.

Fire to my supporters and peace to my enemies

Mared: *A week! Saher must definitely be mad. And what is this weird greeting: Fire to my supporters and peace to my enemies.*

Mared couldn't stand upright. He began to feel dizzy and then he fainted. Minutes later he found himself, as Saher had said, on the thresholds of the kingdom.

The guards at the city gate: Hey, everybody! Mared has come back. He's still alive.

All the commanders, including Darl, approached Mared and started asking him:

"Mared, our great leader, where have you been?"

'We thought you were dead."

"Thank God you have come back safely."

Mared: Darl, how many days have gone by since my disappearance?

Darl: One week, Mared. Where have you been?

Mared: *Oh God! Saher was right. I thought it was just a few hours. Have I gone mad or was it a dream! My God! This is Saher's amulet on the palm of my hand. By God, it's not a dream, but who's going to believe me. They will think that I went crazy after the war.*

Sourfag: Come along, Mared. King Khafan wants to see you.

Mared: Sourfag, why didn't you search for me when I was away for a week?

Sourfag: We did search everywhere, but it was useless. We even sent the exploring jinn to the Cursed City after some soldiers had seen you go into it. However, they didn't find anyone there. Where have you been, Mared?

Mared: They didn't find anyone in the Cursed City?

Sourfag: No. They followed your trail and tried to find you, but to no avail.

Mared: *Should I tell them what happened to me? No, I'll remain silent because it's a secret I have to keep to myself. Is it possible that Saher was telling the truth? He was right so far. My God! What did he do to me and how did he conceal the devils!*

King Khafan: Thank God for your safety, commander of the glorious victory. We have conquered a city today that had always been impossible to conquer in my ancestors' days. We are grateful to God first and then to you, for succeeding in weakening and subduing the enemy. I shall erect a monument in front of my palace to commemorate your victory, Mared. As for the hero, Darl, I shall appoint him as the prince of the Valley of Fire and one of my commanders. So, thank God you're back safe, Mared.

Mared (resuming his conversation with Sourfag and Markhof): I do not really know what happened later to make Khafan banish us. His alibi was that we were conspiring to overthrow him and take over his throne. I was very shocked and depressed by Khafan's decision at that time. He insulted me and deprived me of my military rank and he did the same to you. The six commanders took us and our armies to our exile and we have been here for 300 years. My stay here made me think of Saher's strange talk. How could he foresee everything that he had told me? After much thinking, I decided to take Saher's side and read this amulet because I'm now certain that he had been telling the truth. And that's the reason for my disappearance for a whole week.

Markhof: I don't know what to say to you now, Mared. I'll only believe you if something does happen after you have read the amulet.

Sourfag: Mared, don't forget that we are with you. But would Habel and Nabel be able to get us out of here with our armies?

Mared: I don't know, Sourfag. I'm going to read it now and we'll see what happens. Saher told me that he imprinted the amulet on the palm of my hand and that if I ever want to open it and read it, I should hold up my palm and say: "In the name of God, we conclude." It would then open and a snake would come out of my hand. I must not fear because the orders that I should follow are written on the amulet paper which is inside the snake's mouth. I should cut off the snake's mouth and take the paper and do exactly what I'm ordered to do.

Sourfag: What! How can a snake come out of your hand, Mared?

Markhof: Mared, are you mad? Do you believe what this Saher told you?

Mared: If you had seen what I saw, you would believe him. We have nothing to lose. Let's see what's going to happen.

Mared held up the palm of his hand and said: "In the name of God, we conclude." A strong wind blew in

Mared's chamber. It was so powerful that things started flying about. Then, all of a sudden, it stopped.

Mared felt an excruciating pain in his hand which made him cry out loud. A big snake came out of Mared's hand. Sourfag and Markhof were so scared that they couldn't believe their eyes. They thought they were dreaming. After the snake came out of Mared's hand, he cut off its head and took the amulet from its mouth. His hand started bleeding. He opened the amulet and read:

"Fire to my supporters and peace to my enemies

Great leader, Mared, your time has come now. From the time you read the amulet, the clock will tick, the minutes will strike the seconds and the hours will be reversed. You are now one of my assistants, and your rank is below that of Habel and Nabel. Should you wish to be promoted to a rank higher than Habel's and Nabel's and above King Khorkhis, you must do exactly what I tell you without any question or objection.

Stand up now and raise your hand to the sky and let Markhof and Sourfag do the same. Say out loud: 'Habel and Nabel, we have agreed to the conditions of Saher.' They would soon appear and take care of the matter.

Fire to my supporters and peace to my enemies."

Mared: What do you think, brothers, shall we do as he said?

Markhof: What are his conditions, Mared? It seems that Saher is imposing on us some very hard conditions that we might not be able to fulfill.

Sourfag: Yes, you are right, Markhof. Have you noticed how strange his letter was? Even his greeting doesn't resemble that of someone who believes in God.

Mared: Sourfag, I think he is an infidel. But that doesn't matter as long as he wants to help us.

Sourfag: Mared, what if he requests us to do something that we cannot do? What would happen to us? Would he punish us?

Mared: I don't know, Sourfag. Saher is eccentric. I don't know what he wants and in spite of my wisdom I could never unravel his mysterious personality. But, brothers, suppose that we don't want Saher to help us, how are we going to get out of here? We shall be exiled forever, and I have no doubt that Khorkhis intends to get rid of us while we are here. Saher is our only alternative.

Markhof: So be it! Let's raise our hands and summon Habel and Nabel.

Mared: Does that mean that you agree to Saher's conditions?

Markhof and Sourfag: Yes, we do.

Mared; Then let us execute the first condition.

The three commanders raised their hands to the sky and started calling out to Habel and Nabel in a loud voice. They kept on calling their names but nothing happened. Five minutes later, the sky was transformed into a big black cloud which blocked the sunlight. Rain started pouring and strong winds started blowing. The people of the Forbidden City were startled by this sudden transformation. The guards could not believe their eyes. The storm was striking the city gate and the guards feared that the gate would break from the force of the storm.

Each one of the soldiers was trying to keep the gate from breaking down. Inside the city, some houses were falling apart while others were flying in all directions. Suddenly, the rains and winds stopped and everyone was surprised by this sudden change, especially because the cloud was still over the Forbidden City. The terrified city was transformed, in a very short time, to a ghost city. Each one of the jinn and devils and merdan was crying because of the loss of their homes or their possessions or their children. The city was in a state of confusion. There was no more light to illuminate the streets and the city outline was so radically changed that no one could distinguish where he was. The traps of the city guards were scattered everywhere and the army was dispersed. A state of emergency was declared. At that moment, the three commanders were also frightened. It was such a terrible sight such as they had never seen or heard of before in their world.

The door to Mared's chamber was opened and Habel and Nabel went in.

Habel and Nabel: Peace be upon the followers of God.

Mared: And greetings to you from the believers in God.

Habel and Nabel: A long time ago, we stood in a similar position and you asked us about the Cursed City. Do you remember, Mared?

Mared: Yes, I remember. I asked you about what had happened to the city.

Habel and Nabel: Do you see now what had happened to the Cursed City? The storm today was but a miniature picture of what had happened to the Green City. This is Saher's curse.

Markhof: My God, Sourfag. Can you believe what we have seen today? I swear it's like a dream. Look at these two with their strange clothes and how they have caused the storm!

Sourfag: You were right, Mared. We started to think that you had gone mad when you told us about Habel and Nabel and Saher. I swear I can hear the crying of children and the shouting of women. I can see fathers searching for their children. And all that happened in just a few minutes.

Habel and Nabel: What are you whispering? Tell us.

Sourfag: No, masters. We are just shocked by what happened.

Habel and Nabel: So you have agreed to Mared's conditions. By God, if you renege even on one of them, the consequences will be detrimental to you. To all the conditions you will answer as follows: "We hear and obey."

The three commanders: At your command, our great masters.

Habel and Nabel: Then the first condition is to prepare your armies at this very moment. We want them to take their positions in the palace yard. Get all the war equipment ready as if you were going to fight a decisive battle.

The three commanders: At your command.

The three commanders set about preparing their armies and the war equipment, according to the orders. When they went out of the palace, they were shocked by what they saw. Fires were blazing everywhere; the jinn were wandering about aimlessly as their houses were demolished by the storm. It was such a sorrowful sight. The dead were scattered all around and children were crying over the dead bodies of their mothers and fathers. The whole city became a cursed city. They were very shocked and saddened by what they saw, but, after what they had witnessed, they believed that Habel and Nabel would be able to liberate them. Each of the commanders was telling the other two how they should initiate the attack on the city's gate and what Habel's and Nabel's plans were. It should be a tight plan, though with Habel and Nabel at their side, there would be no plans; only the use of force.

Mared: We did as you ordered, master.

Markhof: How can we break through the gate? Are you going to create another storm?

Habel and Nabel: Who told you that the purpose of these armies is to break through the gate?

Sourfag: Then why did we prepare our armies if we are not going to attack the gate?

Habel and Nabel: No. The gate does not concern us. The purpose of this army is to exterminate all the inhabitants of the Forbidden City.

Mared: What are you saying? Do you want us to kill everyone?!

Habel and Nabel: Yes, everyone. Have no mercy on children, women and the elderly. We want you to behead them all and scatter their bodies across the Forbidden City.

Markhof: And why do you want to kill the women and children? Aren't the men enough for us!

Habel and Nabel: You have agreed to the conditions. If you violate them, you will all die. These are Saher's conditions.

Mared: And why all this bloodshed?

Habel and Nabel: This is a sacrifice to Saher. Anyone who wishes Saher to help him must offer him a sacrifice. This is your offering in return for your escape and glory.

Mared: So he murders a whole city!

Habel and Nabel: You wanted glory. You wanted to become the king of jinn and devils. This is the price; the whole world for the blood of one city. Now answer me, Mared. Do you agree to this condition or shall we murder all of you?

Markhof and Sourfag: Mared, what have we got ourselves into? Now, we have to fulfill the conditions or else we all die. Damn this Saher, how shrewd he is! He put us in a most difficult situation.

Mared: Then let's do what we have been ordered to do; or we shall meet our death.

Sourfag: Mared, there are innocent children in this city; how can we be so heartless as to cut off their heads?

Mared: We have already agreed to the conditions and we must abide by them. From now on, we have to bear the consequences of our actions.

Markhof: If I had known that this would happen, I wouldn't have agreed on summoning Habel and Nabel.

Mared: What's the use now, Markhof! We did what we did and we have no other option.

Habel and Nabel: Don't take too long. We are restricted to a specific timing and then we shall leave. What is your decision?

The three commanders: Your orders will be obeyed.

Habel and Nabel: After you have killed the last person in the Forbidden City, a thick fog will descend on it and then you will find yourselves in the Cursed City. This way, you would have gone out of the Forbidden City. Our mission will have been accomplished and Saher will be giving you further instructions.

Markhof: My God, can they really do that?

Mared: Yes, they can. They moved me from the Cursed City to Khafan's kingdom in the same way.

Sourfag: Master Mared, the armies are waiting for us.

The three commanders went to meet their soldiers and gave them the instructions. The soldiers were shocked by their commanders' instructions, but in the world of jinn, soldiers cannot but obey their leaders even if they were ordered to kill themselves. That was the army regulation. The soldiers swept out of the palace gates and launched a brutal attack on the people of the city. They massacred them all without mercy, without distinguishing between young or old, men or women. The instructions were clear; killing everyone in sight.

They killed them all without pity and cut them off into pieces. In the meantime, one of the flying jinn witnessed the massacre and informed the head guard at the gate. The latter was startled by these actions and called out: "Prepare the army for the counter attack. They will attack the gate any minute now and try to get out. Messenger, go and inform King Khorkhis."

The Kingdom of Khorkhis

Messenger: My master, chamberlain Bilban!

Bilban: What's wrong, messenger? Why do you look so scared?

Messenger: Master, A fierce storm, such as I have never seen before, blew over the Forbidden City. It was so strong that our guards were scattered and the soldiers were dispersed. Even the traps were blown away!

Bilban: What! How did that happen?

Messenger: I don't know. We heard the people of the city screaming for help and because the wind was so strong, we thought that the city gate was going to break down.

Bilban: Come with me now to see the king.

Bilban: My master, King Khorkhis, I have bad news from the Forbidden City.

Khorkhis: What is it, Bilban?

Bilban: The messenger says that a fierce storm blew over that area. He had never seen such a storm before. It was so strong that the armies were scattered and dispersed and the traps were blown away. The gate almost broke down. They heard screams for help coming from the people inside the city. What shall we do, sir?

Khorkhis: A storm! This is very strange. Storms are unusual in that area.

Bilban: What do you want us to do? Shall we send reinforcements?

Khorkhis: I don't know. But this is good news. Perhaps this storm will blow everyone away including the three commanders.

Messenger: Your majesty, there is something else.

Khorkhis: What is it? What happened other than the storm?

Messenger: Yes. We have received a report from one of the guards of the Forbidden City, who is also one of the flying jinn, that the three commanders launched a barbarous attack on the city and massacred all the people.

Khorkhis: My God! What happened to them? Have they gone mad?

Bilban: Your majesty, if we do not stop them, they will attack the gate and escape.

Khorkhis: Bilban, you must warn the kings of the jinn and devils. Send them the report and tell commander Khaji, commander of the Black Devils Army, and commander Sural, commander of the Red Army to come to me immediately.

Bilban: At your majesty's command. They will come immediately.

Khorkhis: Messenger, return to your area and inform them that the reinforcements are on their way. Commanders Khaji and Sural will be leading the Red Army and the Black Devils Army. Tell them to put up as much resistance as they can if the gate is attacked. Fly in peace.

In the meantime, commanders Khaji and Sural arrived and stood before the king. He said: "Great commanders, I have chosen you because you are the strongest and fiercest commanders in wars. A messenger from the Forbidden City has just informed me that Mared and his associates launched a brutal attack on the people of the city and, with their armies, started killing everyone without exception. This action displeases God the Almighty. It also shows their disobedience of the peace treaty. Proceed quickly, with your armies, to the Forbidden City. Take as many soldiers as you want because you are going to face Mared, Sourfag and Markhof; the strongest three among the mutinous commanders. Go now without delay."

Khaji: We shall do what you want, your majesty. However, I have a small suggestion.

Khorkhis: What is it, Khaji?

Khaji: You are aware that Mared is one of the great merdan, and Markhof and Sourfag belong to the sea beasts and ogres. Don't you think we should be three against three?

Sural: Indeed, he's right. There should be a third commander with us because we are going to confront the strongest three.

Khorkhis: No, no. I cannot grant you this request. The state needs them here. You can defeat them. What's wrong with you! Are you afraid of Mared?

Khaji: We are not afraid of Mared. We are just making a suggestion.

Khorkhis: Keep in mind that there is also an army of merdan and ogres and beasts at the gate of the Forbidden City and they will support you. Go on now, we don't have much time.

Khaji and Sural: At your command and service, your majesty, King Khorkhis.

The two commanders headed to the headquarters and started equipping their armies. They left through the kingdom gates towards the Forbidden City with utmost speed. Meanwhile, Khaji asked Sural: "Do you remember what I told you on the day of allegiance?"

Khaji: Yes, I do. You told me that you were seeing bloods flooding the valleys.

Sural: And that's exactly what I had meant then. The bloods have started flowing in the valleys. I can almost smell them from here.

Khaji: What are you saying, Sural? How can you tell if a war will start here! Is it an uneasy feeling or a dream that you had?

Sural: No, Khaji. But I'll tell you a secret. Do you remember when we searched for Mared right after the battle of the Valley of Fire?

Khaji: Yes, I remember. We went to the Cursed City and organized several search teams. How could I forget that day!

Sural: Do you remember a person called Saher?

Khaji: Yes. But this is the legend of the Cursed City.

Sural: I saw him in the Cursed City.

Khaji: Are you out of your mind, Sural! What are you saying?

Sural: When he came up to me and told me he was Saher, I thought I was going out of my mind. I froze in my place. He told me that if Khafan's youngest son came to power and ordered me to kill Mared, Markhof and Sourfag, then I was going to die. He told me to reveal that secret to my close friend who would be accompanying me to murder the three commanders. He advised me to take sides with Mared or else we would lose. Then that Saher disappeared. I couldn't follow him and his speech was very frightening. How could he say that and why would I kill the greatest leader? And who was that person who would go with me?

It is impossible that Khafan would send Mared into exile after his great victory over the Valley of Fire. On the contrary, this victory was going to bring him closer to

Khafan and his family. Many years later, King Khafan ordered the exile of Mared, Markhof and Sourfag after accusing them of treason. I was very scared but my heart was at peace because Saher had told me that when Khafan's youngest son came to power, he would order us to kill them. I thought to myself that I would not live to see that day because the youngest son then was Khorkhis and he had ten brothers who were older than him. However, when King Khafan died and all his sons and brothers also died with the exception of Khorkhis, I swear that I felt very scared of Saher's speech. That's why I didn't say anything when Khorkhis ordered us to kill the three commanders in front of the kingdom gate. Saher's words perplexed me and thus I didn't speak as I was reflecting upon his words. When Khorkhis was discussing his plan with us, I told him that someone was trying to overthrow him. That was a lie so that Khorkhis wouldn't suspect me. Do you know the reason now? He has just ordered us to go and kill Mared and his comrades. I believe that what Saher had said was true and that you are the close friend who should know this secret.

Khaji: You know that what you're saying is very serious, Sural. It seems to me that you intend to disobey Khorkhis' orders.

Sural: That's not what I meant. I swear that Saher's talk drove me mad. I couldn't believe it. It was as if he could foresee future events. I know this is unacceptable in religion, but what is the explanation of all this?

Khaji: I don't know what to say to you, Sural. You should have consulted with Wise Fouta about this. He is a better authority on these matters.

Sural: I'm aware of that. But the wise man hasn't yet come back from the Valley of Worship. I've been waiting for him ever since he left.

Khaji: Sural, We need to use your mastermind. We shall come face to face with the three greatest commanders. Forget about Saher's talk now and think of how we shall make an assault on the city. Maybe Saher had wanted to distort your thoughts.

Sural: Yes, Khaji. I have to clear my mind now. There's a war that I have to lead. I must push Saher's talk out of my mind. I shall never betray my homeland.

Khaji: God bless you, Sural. Come on, we are near the gate.

In the meantime, all the people of the Forbidden City were massacred. The whole city reeked of the odor of blood. The bloods were seeping out under the city gate. The soldiers became very scared upon seeing all that blood. They said: "Oh God! What is happening in there?" The flying jinn brought them the news of an unprecedented massacre in the history of the jinn. All the children's, women's and elderly people's heads were cut off and thrown all across the city which was tinted red by so much blood. To witness such a sight was pure mental torture. After the massacre, only one child was left alive in the Forbidden City. Mared said: "leave him, don't kill him yet."

We shall scare the guards at the gate first.

Soldiers, throw all the heads and body parts outside for the guards at the gates to see. The soldiers did as they were ordered. Five hundred thousand soldiers were catching the body parts and throwing them like pouring rains outside the gate. It was a horrendous sight that frightened the army outside the gate and caused it to disband. King Khorkhis' messenger arrived and informed them that the king was sending commanders Khaji and Sural for the counter-attack. They waited for the commanders to join them with reinforcements, relieved with the impending arrival and support of two of the six commanders. Mared and his comrades persisted in throwing out the body parts until the ground was completely covered with corpses. Then, Mared cut off the child's head and threw it outside the wall. After killing the last person, the city was quiet. All its inhabitants had been massacred and only the army outside the gate was spared. In the silence, only the shrieks of predatory birds that had come to devour the corpses were heard. Fog descended on the city and the army that consisted of five hundred thousand soldiers disappeared.

The two commanders arrived at the gate. They were surprised by the unusually thick fog. They could not see anything. Some of the guards that had fled the scene came back when they saw the commanders and thanked God that they themselves were still alive.

Sural: Guards, why are you so frightened? What is this fog?

Guard: Commander, there was fierce fighting inside and we heard the screams of women and children. The soldiers spared no one.

Khaji: Where are the flying jinn? I want them to report to me immediately.

The flying jinn: Sir, the soldiers of Mared and his comrades have totally destroyed the city and murdered all the people. Bloods flowed like rivers. Look at the ground, sir.

Sural: My God! Look Khaji, This place is full of blood.

Khaji: Woe to them! How could they have done such a horrible thing?

The flying jinn: They were not satisfied with all that killing; they also threw the corpses outside to scare the guards at the gate.

Sural: Oh, what happened to your heart, Mared!

Khaji: Sural, what do we do now? All the people died and most of the soldiers have fled. What can we do with this thick fog? We cannot overpower them under these circumstances.

Sural: Flying jinn, take us to the gate. We cannot see anything here in this fog.

The flying jinn cleared the way for them. As they approached the gate, they saw the corpses scattered everywhere. They were shocked by that eerie, agonizing sight. There were bodies of old people, women and children everywhere. The soldiers were afraid too. Khaji said: "Look, Sural, we have never seen anything like that since the great wars. And even then, women and children were not slaughtered! This is a massacre that no jinn's heart can tolerate. What has come over Mared and his comrades?" The army lined around the gate and Khaji gave his orders for readiness. He also dispatched the flying jinn to King Khorkhis to submit the report.

Sural: What do we do now, Khaji? I swear to God I cannot think of any plan after what I have seen. The situation here has changed. My God, this city has become a cursed city.

Khaji: You are right, Sural. The fog and silence have turned it into a cursed city. We shall wait for Khorkhis' instructions.

Sural: What did you write to Khorkhis in your report?

Khaji: I wrote exactly what I have seen. I described to him the massacre that has taken place.

Sural: Did you tell him that we are not well prepared?

Khaji: Are you mad, Sural? Do you want us to degrade our standing? What would Khorkhis think of us? The strongest two of his six commanders; commander of the Black Devils and commander of the Red Army are scared!

Sural: I'm not talking about fear, Khaji. I'm talking about preventing bloodshed.

Khaji: That's what Mared wanted. We shall teach him a lesson he would never forget. Don't worry, my friend. Remember that I am one of the devils and you are one of the red jinn. We are tough and our armies are very strong. We shall do what Khorkhis demands of us. Let's wait for the messenger that we have sent to bring us Khorkhis' reply.

The messenger reached the palace of King Khorkhis at breakneck speed. He said to the king: "Your majesty, this is a report from Commander Khaji. They are besieging the Forbidden City at the moment."

King Khorkhis: Messenger, read out the report. But before you do, Bilban, I want all the commanders to come and listen.

Bilban: Yes, your majesty.

The four commanders came hurriedly because they knew that it was Khaji and Sural's report. That was a very big and crucial battle and everyone was fearful of its outcome. In addition to that, they were all united in their disagreement with the king's decision to send only two to confront three; and not any three, but the strongest three. The commanders entered the king's chamber and saw the messenger standing before the king. The king ordered them to stand beside him and the messenger started reading the report:

"In the name of the immortal king, God the Almighty
I write to your majesty with blood and with the breaths of the martyrs. My master, King Khorkhis, I send you the greeting of a believer in God.

Peace to all who follow the light of God. Your majesty, the conditions here have changed. The ground is colored

red by the spilt blood. Mared and his companions killed all the inhabitants of the Forbidden City. And as if it wasn't enough for them to kill women and children, they also threw the dead bodies outside the city walls. The guarded area has become the scene of a massacre that I have never witnessed throughout my whole military career. The jinn world too has never known such a massacre. The area is quiet; you can only hear the shrieks of predatory birds feeding on the dead bodies. Fog covers the whole place preventing us from seeing our own hands. The whole region resembles the Cursed City. Many guards were so scared that they fled away from the gate. The region is terrorized. If we hadn't found some flying jirn, we wouldn't have recognized the Forbidden City. It has been transformed. What are your orders now, sir? We shall wait for your reply.

And peace upon the followers of God"

King Khorkhis: Is it true what we heard? Is the situation as gruesome as described?

Bilban: Master, I suggest you send them the reinforcements now.

King Khorkhis: By God, no! I am not going to send them any more reinforcements. I shall not give Mared more than his worth.

Bilban: As you have heard, sir, the situation is extremely bad. If we don't make a move, there will be a disaster.

King Khorkhis: What do you think, commanders?

Commander Torn: I agree with Bilban. One of us must go to support them.

Commander Fifgel: think I should go, sir. My soldiers, the flying jinn, would be of much help to them.

Commander Shuja: Sir, we are four of your strongest commanders. Choose one of us.

Commander Darl: You know, sir, that Mared is very strong and clever. I think you had better send two.

King Khorkhis: Why are you all so afraid of Mared? Remember that he's going to face two of my strongest commanders. He could not hold out. Khaji's army alone is enough, and Sural is his reinforcement. Messenger, I shall give you the parchment. Wait for my reply.

The four commanders sensed the seriousness of the situation. They knew that Mared was very powerful, but King Khorkhis underestimated his power because he had never accompanied him in a war. They started whispering among themselves, *What if Mared and his companions defeat Khaji and Sural! We shall be in an unenviable situation. The king should have sent one of us. King Khafan, God have mercy on his soul, would have acted differently.*

The king came out of his private chamber and gave the messenger the text of the letter. He addressed the commanders: "Get ready, all of you, war is imminent! Commander Fifgel, I want to send you on a mission. You will go to the Valley of Worship and bring Wise Fouta back with you, but not right now. I'll wait for the second report from Khaji and Sural to tell me the outcome of the battle. Take this parchment which is stamped by my personal seal. It is the emergency seal. Give it to Wise Fouta. And you, Darl, take this parchment with the emergency seal on it too and deliver it to the kingdom of the five devils without delay. You, Torn, go to the kingdom of the jinn and give them this parchment with the emergency seal without delay. Shuja, I want you to stay here to protect the kingdom in case of any contingency. Do you all understand my instructions? Go now with my blessings."

Each commander left to execute his orders with the utmost speed. That was the first state of emergency during the reign of King Khorkhis.

The Forbidden City

The king's messenger reached Khaji and Sural and handed them the king's parchment. Khaji read the single line inscribed on it:

Peace be upon you,

Kill them in the same way they killed their people. Have no mercy on any of them. I want the heads of Mared, Sourfag and Markhof now.

Khaji: Sural, what kind of a letter is this?

Sural: I don't know, Khaji, but these are the king's orders. He wants us to storm the gate and kill them without taking any prisoners.

Khaji: So, what is the plan now?

Sural: This is the plan. Listen, Khaji, your army of devils is characterized by its strength and mine by its speed. Mared's soldiers are high jumpers while Sourfag's soldiers are well known for their treachery. As for Markhof, his army of ogres is extremely powerful. We should make the best of these characteristics.

Khaji: What shall we do then?

Sural: We shall divide the army into four divisions:

The first division will consist of the Black and Red Armies.

The second division will consist of the Black Army only.

The third division will consist of the Red Army only.

The fourth division will be under our joint command.

The first division will be in the forefront. The speed of my army will overwhelm Mared's army and allow your soldiers to kill them. But first they will have to lure them outside as fighting inside the city will be hindered by the houses. Mared and his associates are familiar with the internal area, and this will gain them power. Thus we shall give instructions for the first division to try and lure them to leave the city by employing the scheme of deceptive retreat. As for the second and third divisions, they would hide on the sides and, as soon as Mared and his associates come out, they will surround them and kill them. The fourth division, which is ours, will keep a watchful eye on Mared and his associates' moves to see what they intend to do. Then, we attack them and cut off their heads. If the three commanders are murdered, their armies would be defeated and would try to flee. Khaji, we must execute the plan as it is. Any mistake will bring us defeat. Do you understand?

Khaji: It's a good plan, Sural. But with this thick fog, how can we fight a battle when we cannot see clearly?

Sural: That's why the army will be led by the flying jinn. They will be their guides. Khaji, go now and give the instructions to the soldiers. Whoever violates them will meet his death.

Thereafter, Khaji proceeded to give the instructions and start organizing the army lines. In the meantime, the fog lifted a little and visibility was better than before. Sural and Khaji were pleased with the change as it would facilitate their mission. Afterward, Sural changed his insignia to the red color while Khaji changed his to the black color. When commanders changed their insignias, it meant that they intended to be most ferocious and ruthless. Changing indicated power and the intensity of the ensuing fighting. They were not going to underestimate their enemies at all. Drums and bugles signaled the start of the war.

The guards opened the gate and attacked. The first division of Khaji and Sural's armies entered the city and, to their great astonishment, found it deserted.

The chief of Khaji's army: What is this? Where are Mared and his comrades?

The chief of Sural's army: I don't know. Look at the destruction in this city!

The chief of Khaji's army: Could this be a plot?

The chief of Sural's army: I don't think so. Where an army of five hundred thousand soldiers could be hiding?

The chief of Khaji's army: I don't know. They could have escaped, but how? How could the guards at the gates not have seen them!

The chief of Sural's army: I shall go myself and inform the two commanders.

The chief hurriedly traversed the army lines to report to his commanders. They were shocked by his tale and did not believe him. They thought it was a scheme of Mared's. Sural said: "Our plan will not work out anymore. We shall all enter the city. It's a matter of life or death."

Khaji: Let's go to their castles then! We might find them there. Soldiers, be ready to attack! Sural, you go to the castles of Markhof and Sourfag while I go to Mared's castle. Let everyone be prepared for any eventuality! Go with God's blessing.

The army separated into two groups. Khaji headed towards Mared's castle while Sural headed towards Markhof and Sourfag's castle. Khaji reached Mared's castle and barged in. His soldiers searched everywhere but did not find anyone. Khaji went to Mared's chamber but found nothing. He was very surprised. He wondered how they could all have escaped! "Guard, you are better informed about the city's entrances and exits. Is there any other gate or exit?" he asked.

The guard answered: "No, master. The city has only one entrance and exit. We kept our watch even when most of our guards had fled. No one went out and I don't think there's another exit. Even if there was one, we would have heard their sounds upon leaving. Remember, master, these are three commanders with their troops. How could we have not seen or heard them?"

Khaji ordered an extensive search of the castle in the hope of finding some of Mared's servants. After a long search, no one was found. Even the servants had all been murdered! Khaji then gave instructions to leave and sent a messenger to Sourfag and Markhof's castle to report to Sural.

In the meantime, Sural had reached the castle and found no one. It was completely empty. The ground was covered with the bloods of the murdered servants of Markhof and Sourfag. Sural had also searched all the chambers thorough y and found nothing. He was worried that it could be a plot of Mared's, but could not explain how a whole army could disappear!

Khaji's messenger arrived and read Khaji's report to Sural. Sural joined Khaji at the gate and asked him, "Khaji, what should we do now?"

Khaji: I don't know! How can a whole army disappear?

Sural: Could there be other exits that we don't know about?

Khaji: No. I have dispatched ten of my best trackers and they found nothing. The city is tightly guarded and there is only one exit. They didn't even find any traces of the escaping soldiers. But they saw something suspicious. All the traces that they found were located in the same spot.

The weird thing was that they hadn't moved from there on. It was like they had been swallowed by the earth!

Sural: Is there a logical explanation to all this? Could this be Saher's doing?

Khaji: How can Saher do that? Do you think he has the power to make armies disappear? What are you hinting at, Sural? Have you gone mad?

Sural: I swear by God that it is Saher. What shall we do now: stay here or send a messenger to Khorkhis?

Khaji: I suppose we should send a messenger and remain here. Perhaps we will find an answer.

Khaji sent the messenger with a report to King Khorkhis. When he arrived, the king was standing alone. Aside from Shuja and Fifgel, no one was beside him. The messenger told him: "Great King Khorkhis, I have Khaji's report."

Khorkhis: Read it out now.

The messenger:

"Peace be upon the followers of God,

My master, king Khorkhis, I send you this report neither to announce our victory nor to inform you of our failure. I am writing to you with a very confused mind.

Your majesty, we entered the city as invaders, but were startled by the absence of Mared and his comrades and their troops. We have no theories on where they could be. We searched their castles and chambers and found no one. We entered the armies' quarters but found nothing and no one. We sent trackers in their pursuit but they could not find any traces of them. Their traces stopped at a spot near the gate, where it seemed they all disappeared from the face of the earth.

What should we do now, master? Should we return or wait for your instructions?

Greetings to the followers of God."

King Khorkhis was perplexed by the report. He couldn't believe what he had heard. He asked the messenger if it was true. The messenger answered: "Your majesty, everything mentioned in this report is true. By God, the city now resembles the Cursed City."

Khorkhis: But where did Mared and his associates go? How could they disappear? I know the Forbidden City. It has only one entrance and exit and it's surrounded by traps. How could they vanish like that? We must wait for Wise Fouta. He will provide us with an answer. We only have one solution. Messenger, go and tell them to return immediately and lock the city gate. Let them place more soldiers to guard the gate. Proceed with your utmost speed.

Commander Shuja: Your majesty, you do realize the gravity of this report.

Khorkhis: Yes I do, Shuja. But how did they disappear and where did they go?

Shuja: Your majesty, do you suspect treason?

Khorkhis: I think so. Otherwise, how were they able to get out if not with the support of some of the guards?

Shuja: I don't think so, master. How could the guards do such a thing? And even if they did, they cannot all be traitors. Something weird has taken place.

Khorkhis: Where is Fouta? I'm going out of my mind. If Mared and his associates have escaped, it means that great wars will break out. Shuja, where is chamberlain Bilban?

Shuja: He's in the palace yard reading out the instructions to the soldiers.

Khorkhis: I swear by God that I can smell high treason. I must recount the dream to Wise Fouta now. Fly, Fifgel, at your maximum speed to the Valley of Worship and bring Wise Fouta back immediately!

The Valley of Worship

It was called 'The Valley of Worship' because it was inhabited solely by the good and wise jinn who held worship and prayer sessions there. It was also called 'The Valley of Peace' because there was never any war there since the creation of the jinn. Father Sumia, father of all the jinn, reigned over this valley. Sumia was the creator of the entire jinn dynasty and he was one of the good, immortalized individuals whom God favored among his worshippers. The jinn feared but respected him as he was their original father and they were his descendants. However, Sumia did not interfere a lot with the jinn's matters. He was always occupied with his own worship rituals and religious activities.

Fouta went to the Valley of Worship to gain wisdom from the wise and enrich his sagacity and knowledge of theology. Fouta was very intelligent and well-versed in worldly and religious matters. Pupils competed with each other for the purpose of gaining some of his knowledge. Fouta was very close to Father Sumia and at the time, they were discussing a certain issue when the good chamberlain told them: "My master, Father Sumia, one of King Khorkhis' commanders is requesting permission to enter."

Sumia: Who is that commander?

Chamberlain: It is Fifgel, commander of the flying jinn.

Sumia: Fifgel! This is strange. Why would Khorkhis send Fifgel over here?

Chamberlain: Fifgel says it's a very urgent matter. He requests permission to talk to Wise Fouta.

Fouta: To talk to me? It is strange indeed! There must be an emergency.

Sumia: All right chamberlain. Show him in.

Chamberlain: At your command, Father Sumia.

Sumia: This is very strange. Why would Fifgel want to see you, Fouta?

Fouta: I don't know, master. But I suppose something serious has happened.

Fifgel entered the palace of Father Sumia and greeted him and Wise Fouta: "Eternal peace upon you, Father Sumia and eternal peace upon you, Wise Fouta. I apologize for interrupting your worship and prayer sitting. But I swear by God that I only came here to inform you about a grave incident that might change our history and cause much bloodshed among innocent people. Khorkhis sent me here to accompany Wise Fouta back to the kingdom with the utmost speed. He has declared a state of emergency and readiness."

Fouta: Is that possible, Fifgel? What happened? Tell us.

Fifgel: Mared and his associates revolted in the Forbidden City and massacred its entire population. The victims' bloods seeped outside the city gates. Not only that, but they murdered women, children and old people, cut them into pieces and threw them outside the city. It has become a ghost city. King Khorkhis ordered the execution of Mared and his associates and sent Sural and Khaji for that purpose. However, when they entered the city, they didn't find anyone at all; neither the commanders nor their armies. They had suddenly disappeared without trace. The city is completely deserted. We think that Mared escaped but we don't know how!

Fouta: Escaped? How could he get away with guards surrounding the place?

Fifgel: Master, I don't know how they escaped but Khorkhis dispatched the rest of the commanders to the jinn and devils' cities to alert them.

Sumia: I know how they escaped.

Fouta: How, Father?

Sumia: It is Saher.

Fifgel: But how, master? Saher is just a legend.

Fouta: How can Saher make a whole army disappear, Father?

Sumia: No, Fifgel. Saher is real. He is not a legend. He is also capable of doing much more than that. I shall tell you Saher's story.

The Story of Saher

Saher used to live in the Green city which is now known as the Cursed City. He was one of the jinn descended from the devils. Saher was famous for his tricks and wizardry. He became the most reputed wizard in the Green City. His tricks were very original, smart and complicated. No one was ever able to outdo him. He became the 'talk of the town'. He was very popular in his city. One day, Saher was afflicted with a severe illness which rendered him incapable of pursuing his hobby. His illness got worse and, people who used to gather around him in admiration, now avoided him. One of the sheikhs of the jinn advised him to recite the praises of God in the hope of recovering from his disease. Saher followed his advice and the sheikh recited God's praises to him as well. Nevertheless, Saher could not tolerate his illness. The sheikh told him: "Do not be sad, Saher, when God loves a person He puts him to test." Saher answered: "I want life, not death. I want life, sheikh. What is the price of life? Is there a price for life?" The sheikh answered: "Don't ask for life, Saher, for God will deprive you of the bliss of the after-life. God's paradise is in the afterlife. It is superior to life and everything in it." Saher retorted, "I ask for life."

The sheikh then said: "I beg you to seek God's forgiveness, Saher. What you are saying is very serious. Ask for God's forgiveness so that He would not punish you." Saher answered: "Sheikh of the jinn, I have told you that I love life and I want nothing else."

The sheikh left Saher's room, asking for God's forgiveness. At sunrise, Saher started feeling much better and he recovered from his illness completely. It was as if he had never been ill. Saher was surprised by that strange feeling and he regained his energy with amazing speed. The sheikh visited him and said: "Thank God for your recovery, Saher."

Saher: Didn't I tell you, sheikh, that life loves me and it made me well again because I asked for it.

Sheikh: You crazy man! Don't you believe in God?

Saher: I read out the praises of God a lot but I didn't recover. When I asked for life, my health returned.

Sheikh: Saher, don't step out of line. Renew your belief in God.

Saher: I bear witness that Allah is my one and only God.

Sheikh: I hope that you would carefully consider your words before uttering them.

Saher resumed practicing his tricks but by then, he had two new competitors, Habel and Nabel. Their tricks were much better than his; they were incredible. They could hide things and then bring them back. Saher tried to imitate them but he failed. He wasn't able to know their secret. He asked them to teach him their tricks but they refused. He decided to eavesdrop on them to learn their secret but to no avail. Afterwards, Saher began performing tricks that were more original than theirs to regain his popularity. He also went to a friend of his—called Kahen—and told him about Habel and Nabel and their expertise. Kahen said to him: "There's someone called Mushawaz (conjuror). I heard that he was the one who taught Habel and Nabel those tricks." Upon hearing that, Saher became impatient and asked Kahen to take him to the conjuror's house. They went in.

Mushawaz: Who are you, stranger?

Saher: I am Saher, the most famous wizard in the Green City.

Mushawaz: And who's that man standing beside you?

Kahen: I am Kahen, Saher's friend.

Mushawaz: What do you want from me?

Saher: I heard that you were the one who taught Habel and Nabel the trick of hiding things and then bringing them back. I want you to teach me how to perform this trick and others—just like you taught Habel and Nabel.

Mushawaz: How much will you pay me if I do it?

Saher: I don't have much money but I'll try to give you what you want.

Mushawaz: But, can you give me what I want?

Saher: Yes, I will, provided you teach me much better tricks than those you taught Habel and Nabel.

Mushawaz: Then go over to that house. You will find one of the ogres' sheikhs. He's going to give a speech. Go there and listen to him and, when he finishes, come back and tell me what you have learnt.

Saher: Your demand can be easily fulfilled.

Mushawaz: I haven't finished with my demands yet. This is just the first one.

Saher and Kahen headed to the designated house and listened to the sheikh's speech about the power of God. The sheikh was saying that God had great powers that no one could equal. God was generous, strong, mighty and merciful. We should worship Him and only Him. When God loves one of his servants, He puts him to test. However, if that servant asks for life instead of the after-life, he would lose everything. God would grant him life but deny him the afterlife because God is just and no one and nothing can match His justice.

Saher: Do you know, Kahen, this sheikh's speech reminds me of the illness that almost killed me.

Kahen: How?

Saher: When I said that I wanted life and not the after-life, I was completely cured.

Kahen: Is it possible? It seems that when the sheikh of the jinn read God's praises over your body, his reading was a cure.

Saher: Not at all. The sheikh of the jinn could not do anything. Let's go back to Mushawaz, Kahen. The sheikh has finished with his speech.

Saher and Kahen went back to Mushawaz and told him that the speech was finished. He asked: "And what did you learn from it?" Saher answered: "That if we ask for life, we get it." Mushawaz ushered them in. His house was very strange and a foul odor emanated from it. There were dead animals everywhere. Kahen asked him: "What is this awful smell, Mushawaz?"

Mushawaz: Forget the smell and tell me, are you ready to fulfill my demands?

Saher: Yes, I'm ready.

Mushawaz: What about you, Kahen? Do you want to learn?

Kahen: Yes, I do.

Saher: So, Mushawaz, what is your request?

Mushawaz: Saher and Kahen, listen carefully to what I'm going to say. I shall teach you one of the secrets of life. Once you get into this science, you can never get out of it. Do you understand?

Saher: What do you mean?

Mushawaz: I mean that you will be my pupils and you will never disobey my orders. If you disobey me, you will die.

Kahen: Die? What sort of orders are these that will bring our death if we disobey them!

Mushawaz: Listen to me. I see sincerity in your eyes. You really want to learn. I don't teach tricks, Saher. I teach facts.

Saher: What do you mean by facts? Aren't these wizardry tricks?

Mushawaz: No, Saher. They are facts. Listen, my pupils, I asked you to go to the sheikh's lecture because I've been there before and I did what he said and my request was fulfilled.

Saher: And it happened to me too when I was sick. Do you mean, Mushawaz, that when I want to perform a trick I should ask for life and not for God?

Mushawaz: Look, Saher, when you ask for life, you would be disobeying God and your request would be fulfilled because you would have already abandoned your afterlife. Religion should be involved in our actions.

Kahen: Religion! Religion is not about disobeying God!

Mushawaz: This science is new to me. I experimented several times in different situations but I didn't succeed. Then I came up with an idea. I wanted something to happen to me, but I didn't want to ask God to make it happen. Then sacrifice came to my mind.

Kahen: Sacrifice is slaughtering for God. What do you mean then when you say sacrifice?

Saher: Mushawaz, this is blasphemy.

Mushawaz: When you choose this route, you must offer sacrifice. You have come here to sacrifice and there's no going back. You have given me your oath.

Saher and Kahen: And we are going to keep it.

Mushawaz: Then, sacrifice will be in this manner: You bring any animal and offer it as sacrifice in the name of the thing that you want. After that, your request will be fulfilled.

Kahen: Would it be fulfilled so quickly?

Saher: But, Mushawaz, what if it didn't?

Mushawaz: You offer a bigger sacrifice.

Saher: What do you mean, Mushawaz?

Kahen: You mean we sacrifice one of the jinn?!

Mushawaz: That's right, Kahen. We do it if we have to. But when we sacrifice one of the jinn, we take his blood, drink it and smear our body with it and we relieve ourselves in the open, where we are. I'll tell you the reason when the time comes.

Saher: But, Mushawaz, this is dirtiness.

Mushawaz: I know, but playing by these rules will get you what you desire. I tried other methods but with this particular one I got what I wanted. That's why you smelled a foul odor when you entered my house.

Kahen: And what was it you wanted, Mushawaz?

Mushawaz: I wanted power. I wanted to achieve my goal in order to be the most superior among my people in that domain.

Saher: By God, this is a strange science but it's a fine one. So, what do you want us to do today, Mushawaz?

Mushawaz: You asked me to teach you the secret of Habel and Nabel's trick. So, I will. Saher, take this pigeon and offer it as a sacrifice to get what you want. Take the pigeon's blood, smear your body with it and drink it. Then cut the pigeon in two halves. Burn one half and take its ashes and wrap the other half with tree leaves and bury it.

Saher: Why do all that, Mushawaz? What good would come out of it?

Mushawaz: I have trained myself to do these things and pondered about them a lot for a long time. It took me 200 years to think in this manner. Now I need pupils to follow in my steps. You two have come to me and so did Habel and Nabel. You are learning something that took me 200 years of reflecting and experimenting. I passed on my knowledge to you in a few minutes. Look, Saher and Kahen, when we don't slaughter for the sake of God, we have to mention God's name.

Saher: Mention God's name? How can we do that when we are not slaughtering for His sake?

Mushawaz: These are the rituals of this process. You must mention God during the slaughter even though you're doing it for someone other than Him. You disobey God and you get what you desire. This is because you have sold yourselves and your after-life. Thus the entire life would be yours and you shall commit every sin from slaughter to impurity and so on. Do you understand now why I told you to drink the blood of the sacrificed animal and smear your bodies with it? All this is sinful and displeases God. This act of ours depends on committing sins. When you slaughter for someone other than God—as you did in the case of the pigeon—this pigeon will acquire bizarre characteristics. Now I shall explain to you why we cut it in two halves. The first half that we burn turns into ashes. Ashes resemble the soil of the earth but they weigh less. Thus, if we bury these ashes in the earth, they disappear but they remain there even though we cannot see them no matter how closely we look. That's how we gain the power of disappearance. It means that if you sprinkle the ashes over the thing that you want to conceal and cover it with your hands and then uncover it, it would disappear. The reason why we smear our body with the blood and then drink it is to keep some sort of communication between ourselves and the dead pigeon to possess the power of disappearance.

Saher: So that's what Habel and Nabel were doing?

Mushawaz: Indeed. The rule that I'm teaching you must comply with the rule of nature and be its equivalent.

These are the equations.

The first equation:

The properties of ash are similar to those of soil, thus ash equals the soil of the earth; when they are mixed together, the ash disappears in the soil and no one can spot it, but it's still there; therefore, when we bury something, its ashes will disappear from sight but still exist.

This is the first equation, and this is the secret of concealing things. This is the usefulness of the first burnt half of the pigeon. As for the second half, it would complete the equation and bring back the concealed thing. So here is the second equation.

Second equation:

Burying the dead in the earth equals the resurrection of the dead from the earth on the Day of Judgment; therefore, bringing the buried and concealed thing back equals the return of the thing that was concealed.

This is the secret of the disappearance equation. The equation should have two sides in order to achieve what you want. If we do the first action without doing the second, we would not be able to bring the concealed thing back. That is the reason for dissecting the pigeon in two halves; we burn one half and take its ashes and we bury the other half to balance the equation. Do you get it now?

Kahen: What a bizarre and complicated equation! How did you come up with this idea?

Saher: But, Mushawaz, does this equation apply to everything?

Mushawaz: I don't know. I have been trying for 200 years to find the correct method and equation to make things disappear. Now I know it. So this is the secret of disappearance. This secret would also be the key to other new things that we learn. You are now my pupils. I have given you the key and the equation as well, so try to discover new things. It's your turn to help me come up with other unprecedented acts.

Saher: Believe me, Mushawaz; I shall discover more exciting things.

Greatly astonished, Saher and Kahen left Mushawaz while discussing what they had learnt.

(That was how the world of conjuration and magic, as we know it in our modern times, started. These acts were named after Mushawaz and Saher. Mushawaz is the Arabic word for conjuror, and Saher is the Arabic word for magician)

Saher was thinking to himself that he should come up with other new ideas to outdo Habel and Nabel. At the same time, Kahen was reflecting on how he could beat Saher in that science. Each one of them was trying to create new acts in accordance with the equation given to them. It was hard to find the required information. They should find elements that were similar. After many failed attempts, Saher said to himself, *there must be a specific rule to this equation; the equation alone is insufficient.* So he started to search for a rule for the equation and ended up by setting his own rule. In the meantime, Kahen was trying to add new things to the equation until he came up with an idea. When they finished their brainstorming, the two met and went to see Mushawaz.

Mushawaz: Why are you so late?

Saher and Kahen: We do apologize, sir. But we have been thinking of new additions to the equation.

Mushawaz: And have you found any?

Saher: I have, sir.

Kahen: And I have too.

Mushawaz: Speak up, Saher. What have you found?

Saher: In your equation, sir, you used the earth element which is characterized by burial, disappearance and reappearance. After much thinking and trying to find other earth equations, I thought, *why use only the earth element*. Earth is one of life's elements. Thus I divided the elements into four main ones; the ones that form our world.

1- The Earth Element
2- The Water Element
3- The Fire Element
4- The Air Element

By using these four elements, we can form too many equations. Notice, sir, that all these elements complement each other. The earth element needs water for the plants to live. We need air to breathe. Fire provides us with light and, if there's no air, there would be no fire. Do you notice the connection between these four elements? These elements will help us form so many equations.

Mushawaz was amazed at Saher's intelligence and thought, *my God, how clever this young man is! How could he think of all this?* Kahen was getting jealous and the rivalry between them heightened. Kahen said, "It is my turn now, sir." Mushawaz replied, "Show us what you have, Kahen."

Kahen: I have done a lot of thinking and, after several attempts, I got an idea. Why don't we use constellations and astronomy in our equations? For example: Virgo, Scorpio, Leo, Pisces and Taurus. These signs are the characteristics of the months. Thus, if we use also constellations, we would be using the elements of the sky as well.

Mushawaz smiled and said to himself, *how smart they are! Habel and Nabel are no match to them. Their idea about using puzzles was good, even excellent. But these two have established the basis of this new science.* To Kahen and Saher, he said: "Well done. By God, you did not disappoint me. Your ideas are original and powerful and I shall put them in my book. Saher, I like your idea of using the elements and yours too, Kahen, about using constellations. That's why I decided to join the two ideas together to establish the new law."

Saher: What law?

Kahen: Do you mean you are going to take our ideas and merge them together?

Mushawaz: Yes, because they are very good. They must be merged together to make them more powerful. The elements that you mentioned, Saher, will be integrated with Kahen's constellations. There is also Habel and Nabel's idea about using puzzles. It's a good one but we shall not use it at the present. We shall link the elements with the constellations and stars and see how the process works.

Saher: What do you mean by that?

Mushawaz: I'm thinking of a process that is more serious than wizardry and tricks, Saher. I want to use it on our people.

Kahen: Are you saying that we do this to our people? How and in what way?

Mushawaz: I had the notion of making one of the jinn disappear and I wanted to try it. I summoned one of them and applied the disappearance equation on him. He disappeared but he is right here among us.

Saher: Can we really do that? This is good news!

Kahen: Good idea, master.

Mushawaz: Come now. Let's try linking the equations. I think we should link the stars with the elements and constellations.

Saher: How do we go about it?

Mushawaz: This is an equation that I shall form now. The star in the sky is known for its immobility. It guides the travelers. This means that we should link the star with the elements in order to locate the person. Afterwards, we identify this person as having a water star or an earth star and so on. Thus, we can locate him.

Constellations are linked to people. Each one of us has his own constellation. That is how we can form the equation.

The first equation:

One of the jinn equals his constellation which is equal to the movement of the star on the day of his birth.

The second equation:

The star in the sky equals one of the four elements, i.e. the star of earth or water or air or fire, which is equal to one of the jinn.

Saher: But this is a very strange equation and different from the disappearance equation. When is it used?

Kahen: Do you mean, Mushawaz, by this equation of yours, that you want to exploit this new science for evil purposes?

Mushawaz: Imagine how many people in this world have problems. They will resort to us for revenge. Thus, we can use the hidden jinn for taking revenge and no one would ever notice.

Thereafter, the three of them embarked on the task of formulating their equations and sharpening their ideas with the participation of Habel and Nabel. Throughout the years, they kept developing their notions until they attained a level that none of the jinn population had ever attained before. They discovered that the stars and the elements and astronomy influence the power of action. A person with a fire star does not resemble another with an earth star. Likewise, a water star is not the same as an air star. Strength differs from one person to another. Some people can accept their physical capabilities while others cannot. They took this observation into consideration and tried to find solutions to these attributes. And finally they did. They continued working on how to conceal the causes of diseases and to change the genes. They almost finished writing their books, and were always coming up with new ideas. They published many books; but most of them were theoretical and were not put into practice. Each one of the theorists was renowned for a certain characteristic. Kahen was known for his theories on astronomy and occultism. Saher excelled in theories on life and death while Mushawaz distinguished himself by his theories on fear, panic and suicide. Habel and Nabel were renowned for their riddles which empowered the acts of the other three.

When all was done, they met and agreed that each one of them would name his book after him.

1- The Book of Saher (His actions were later called magic)

2-The Book of Mushawaz (His actions were later called conjuration)

3- The Book of Kahen (His actions were later called predictions)

4- The Reference Book of Habel and Nabel (An interpretation and simplification of the three books)

5- The Book of Riddles (It was Habel and Nabel's book)

All these five books led to perdition. Their content was the same. They agreed on a basis for all of them and a unified rule through which none of them could harm another.

113

The rules were the following:

1- Using the jinn in their acts henceforth, and offering a monetary reward which consisted of gold and jewelry to the one who accomplishes the mission assigned to him. Failing that, the sentinels of magic, conjuration and prediction would verify if the work was properly done and kill whoever fails in accomplishing his mission.

2- Anyone who comes to them should provide the gold and diamonds needed as a reward to the person who is going to accomplish the required mission. He should also offer a sum of money to Saher, Kahen and Mushawaz and offer a sacrifice to the one he demands a service from. If, for example, he was asking for Saher's services, he should slaughter in the name of Saher and so on. However, the money would be equally distributed among the three of them.

3- The work would be carried out by way of a contract between them and the person who requests their services. The equations, as well as the request of the concerned person, were detailed in the contract. The requester could ask for the death, suffering or illness of a certain person or even the death of his entire progeny. The contract would then be stamped by the requester's blood.

4- The three of them made up the basis of their work. Nothing could be done without their unanimous consent. They linked all their equations with the initial law, which stated that Kahen, Saher and Mushawaz were the initiators of the equation and the executors of all the works. If one of the foundations was shaken, the work would never be executed. Thus, they created an equation which they called the equation of the beginning. It was the first one ever to connect magic, conjuration and prediction together. It controlled all the magic, conjuration and prediction that existed in the world. Without it, nothing could be accomplished.

The equation of the beginning was as follows:

Its basis was the three of them: Kahen, Saher and Mushawaz who were equivalent to the world of magic, conjuration and prediction. Therefore, an agreement sealed by their blood was equal to an agreement sealed by the blood of the requester; therefore equal to the consent of all three of them to execute the work.

They did not write another equation as it had to be a reverse equation and it had to be called, the equation of the end. But they didn't want an end at all.

Those were the established laws during that epoch. Later on, they started promoting their ideas and their business—magic, conjuration, prediction, equations etc.—all of which, up till then, the world of jinn was not familiar with. Many people did not believe them, but those who did, went to them and requested their services. Years later, they became the three most famous men in the Green City, which was later destroyed due to their evil doings. Anyone who wanted to take revenge on someone, no matter how trivial the reason was, would go to them and ask for their help. They caused total chaos in the city. They promoted the idea that they could undo the evil they had caused to someone if he came to them and asked for a cure. Thus, they became very rich. One might wonder how they were able to persuade the jinn to do their dirty work. They used to go to the poor cities and villages and promise to make their inhabitants rich if they agreed to work for them. As a result, they recruited a big number of hidden jinn, merdar, devils and ogres who carried out the missions.

Their work was done in this manner: When someone went to them demanding revenge, all three would show him their books and their contents so that the requester could choose a certain method of killing. For example, if he chose death from a strange, incurable and fatal disease, the one in charge of this disease would embark on that job. He would appoint one of the hidden jinn for that mission. The jinni (singular of jinn, male or female) would then go to the targeted person and implant the disease in his body. The victim would become very ill and weak. If he goes to a doctor, the hidden jinni would go with him to make the medication ineffective, thus causing the patient's condition to worsen leading to his death. Upon finishing the job, the jinni would be rewarded with the gold and jewelry set aside for him in a specified place, which was kept under watch by the sentinels of magic, conjuration and prediction. If the jinni fails in his mission, he would be killed and the treasure would remain in its place until someone else came and finished the job. (That is the secret of the hidden treasures that we hear about in our days. Many people consult the jinn to discover the hiding place of treasures but they can never find them because they are guarded by sentinels.)

Day by day, they improved their acts and acquired their own pupils. They wrote their most powerful and complicated books that even their pupils were not able to put into practice. A very high level in the world of magic, conjuration and prediction was required for anyone who wanted to practice any of their acts. Their most reputed books were the following:

1- The Magic of Puppets.
2- The Black Palace.
3- The Witchery of Gluttony.

4- Prediction and the Biggest Blasphemy.

5- The Magic of Betting.

5- Death Riddles.

Kahen employed the jinn to eavesdrop on the angels. One day, he heard something that didn't please him. He heard that the three of them were destined to enormous suffering. After having owned the world, Kahen started getting his senses back. He felt that life did not have the taste of the after-life. He regretted all their wrongdoings and evil acts of blasphemy and murder of innocent people. He told Mushawaz what he felt, and the latter had the same feeling. They both felt uncomfortable, even after having possessed everything—wealth, palaces and servants. They had an uneasy feeling. They both agreed to go to Saher and ask him to end everything by writing the reverse equation—the equation of the end—and burning all the books that they published and undoing all their acts of magic, conjuration and prediction. They did not want to have any pupils to follow in their steps after their repentance. Since their law stated that no job could be done without the consent of the three of them, it meant that if one refused a job, it would become void.

So they went to Saher's palace. When they entered his chamber, he was busy putting new equations with Habel and Nabel. They said: "Saher, there is something we have to tell you."

Saher: What is it, brothers?

Mushawaz: Kahen and I have agreed to put an end to this science.

Saher: Are you both mad? After we have come so far with our wondrous acts! You want to stop after we have excelled in this science? Why, Mushawaz?

117

Kahen: One of the jinn overheard that our fate is going to be an extremely painful suffering. Saher, we have owned the world and everything in it and have become the wealthiest men in the Green City; but I don't feel comfortable anymore.

Saher: How can you say that when the world is ours now?

Mushawaz: Wisdom has nothing to do with possession. All possessions will vanish except God's own possessions. Let us repent, return to God and end it all by writing the second equation; the equation of the end.

Saher: Are you both mad? When we went into this business, we knew that we were disobeying God.

Mushawaz: That we did. But the door to repentance is not closed yet.

Saher: Mine is closed and I don't want to repent. I'm happy with what I'm doing.

Kahen: Forget your pride, my friend. Let's end everything now, before it's too late.

Saher: Do you remember what you told us when we first approached you? You said that backing away or disobedience meant death. That was the condition you imposed on us.

Mushawaz: I am your mentor and I'm telling you that I'm taking back my words. Come now, Saher, let's finish with this business and the science that we founded and ask for God's forgiveness.

Saher: I gave you my answer, Mushawaz. I'm not repenting.

Kahen: You are aware that you cannot do anything without our consent. This is our basic rule.

Saher: If you do not leave now, I'm going to kill you. Do you understand? Go ahead and repent but I'm not going to.

Mushawaz: This is my last advice to you, Saher. If you do not agree, Kahen and I will declare war against you.

Saher: Then war it is! I have my two assistants, Habel and Nabel.

Mushawaz and Kahen left. Mushawaz said: "You and I will invalidate the ecuation of the beginning by putting the equation of the end." Kahen then asked him how they could go about it without Saher's consent.

Mushawaz: We must be very well prepared. Saher is at war with us and you know how clever he is. Listen, Kahen, we shall repent first but later we have to face the magic of Saher and the riddles of Habel and Nabel with my conjuration and your power of prediction.

Kahen: Mushawaz, how can we do that when our previous contracts with the jinn, merdan, devils and ogres haven't been executed yet? We promised to pay them with gold upon completing their assignments. How can we breach the contracts? They will side with Saher.

Mushawaz: We shall not breach the contracts. We shall assign them a bigger mission.

Kahen: I suppose you're going to turn the magic on Saher.

Mushawaz: That's right, Kahen. We shall do the mirror equation and turn Saher's magic on him.

Kahen: How can we come up with an equation right now when Saher is preparing his magic to confront us? We don't have enough time.

Mushawaz: I have already thought of the equation and it is written in my book 'The Black Palace'.

It is the following:

The three foundations, Mushawaz, Saher and Kahen are equivalent to a water star and a fire star and an earth star, i.e. equal to the first equation which is the union of the three elements. Therefore, installing the mirror is equal to reversing the task on the taskmaster.

This way, everything will be reversed; so objection means consent. We shall get Saher's consent without his knowledge and against his will. Afterward, we shall finish the equation of the beginning with that of the end, which I have linked with the mirror equation as follows:

Equation of the end is based upon the three foundations, Saher, Mushawaz and Kahen who control the world of magic, conjuration and prediction. Stamping the equation with the foundations' blood would be equivalent to stamping it with the requester's blood following the consent of the three foundations. The mirror equation and the reversing of Saher's magic would cause an imbalance in the three foundations and their words will be reversed, thus leading to the equation of the end which is the same as the end of the beginning.

Kahen: What amazing ideas, Mushawaz. How did you think of such an equation?

Mushawaz: I had to consider it in case one of us turns against another. This equation would apply on the revolting party.

Kahen: But, Mushawaz, this means Saher's death.

Mushawaz: Yes, it does. It is either his death or ours if we fail.

Kahen: Then we must be extremely cautious.

Mushawaz: Kahen, go ahead and inform the prediction soldiers of their new mission and I shall inform the conjuration soldiers of theirs. We shall make use of my book 'The Black Palace' as well as your book 'Prediction and the Biggest Blasphemy'.

Kahen: Don't you need your book 'The Conjuration of Gluttony'?

Mushawaz: No, because that one depends on the passing of years, whereas 'The Black Palace' has a quick and instantaneous effect.

Kahen: Then let's get the army ready. One of my soldiers told me that Saher has started gathering troops with the help of Habel and Nabel. We must set up the confrontation equations. Come on, Mushawaz, we are short of time.

Saher also started setting up his equations with Habel and Nabel's assistance. He told them that Mushawaz was the basis of these acts, as he was the founder of that particular science. He should not be underestimated at all. He requested his two books, 'The Magic of Puppets' and 'The Magic of Betting'.

Habel and Nabel: But, Saher, how can you defeat two of the foundations when you're on your own?

Saher: I must find a new equation which is more powerful than theirs. I am certain that Mushawaz is setting up his own equations to defeat me. I shall try to do something that I have thought of before.

Saher started formulating equations from his books, 'The Magic of Puppets' and 'The Magic of Betting'. Then he had a new idea which was also destructive. His new equation required too many sacrifices and the shedding of innocent people's blood. He named it 'the curse of Saher'.

That curse was characterized by the total and quick destruction of anyone who challenged Saher. The curse would remain in the area that Saher had put a spell on so that every living creature in it would perish, until the time he used the other equation to put an end to the curse. His equation was the following:

Saher is the foundation and he is equal to the magic of betting and the magic of blood. The betting is on Kahen and the blood is on Mushawaz. Betting and blood are equal to Saher's curse, which equals the destruction of the area betted on and the killing in sacrifice to Saher's magic. Therefore, Saher would win the bet and the blood, and the curse would remain, and that is equal to the replacement of the other two foundations with new ones; Habel and Nabel.

After finishing the curse equation, Saher consulted Habel and Nabel. They suggested adding a riddle to his equation to make it difficult for Kahen and Mushawaz to unravel it. What they suggested was an imaginary equation. So it would become: The imaginary equation equals Saher's curse equation which is equal to the equation of replacing the foundation; hence, winning the bet.

That was a very easy equation to unravel. However, if Kahen and Mushawaz were able to solve the imaginary equation, the curse would strike them and they would both die.

Saher was impressed by Habel and Nabel's riddles. They implemented the equations and put them into action. They were ready for the challenge. In the meantime, Mushawaz and Kahen were preparing the mirror equation which would turn the magic on the magician himself. That was a very tough challenge. The armies of Saher, Habel and Nabel were on alert as well the armies of Mushawaz and Kahen. Hence, the three foundations were all present which meant they all gave their consent for the tasks at hand. All the equations would be executed with the consent of the three foundations.

The armies came face to face in the midst of the Green City. Mushawaz told Saher: "I shall give you a final warning. You are no match to me."

Saher: I gave you my answer and you are well aware of it, Mushawaz.

Mushawaz: Well then, watch out, Saher!

The hidden soldiers began to appear, but some of them remained concealed and launched a fierce and violent attack. Each one of them was using his magic, conjuration, prediction and riddles to win the battle. Saher took the first step in using the magic of destruction, while Mushawaz was using a counter-conjuration to dissemble his magic. Kahen was solving the riddles of Habel and Nabel. Fighting in the Green City lasted for many days and it was a fierce war. By using their books, they put the city in an unenviable situation. Such a battle was never witnessed before in the world of jinn. They had so many equations to use against each other that it got to be an epic war that even they were fed up with. Saher said to his two assistants: "Get ready for my own curse, Saher's curse." One of the eavesdropping spies overheard this and told Kahen and Mushawaz what he had heard.

Mushawaz: My God, could Saher have mastered this curse!

Kahen: What's wrong? What curse?

Mushawaz: I was once in Saher's palace and we were discussing some magic and conjuration equations when he asked me, "What is the most powerful equation?" and I told him that I didn't know, because all equations were powerful. Then we had this dialogue:

Saher: I have a very good idea although it's hard to implement it.

Mushawaz: What is that idea that is so hard for you to implement?

Saher: My curse.

Mushawaz: Your curse! Do you want to have your own curse?

Saher: Yes. We know that having a curse does not please God. I want my curse to cause total destruction and remain in the cursed place or person until they ask for mercy.

Mushawaz: But, Saher, this is a very serious issue. You must think in a very complex way and invent a very powerful equation to implement it.

Saher: I realize that. But inventing this equation is time-consuming, and I don't have time. Imagine, Mushawaz, what will happen if I can master it. It means the entire cursed area will be ruined and deserted. Every living thing in it would perish and die if they don't ask for my mercy.

That was when Mushawaz realized that if ever Saher possessed his own curse, he could kill everyone without exception. He said to Kahen: "So I thought of inventing a reverse equation and came up with the mirror equation that I have already told you about. You know now why I thought of this equation. I was certain that one of us would revolt against the others. Force and power spoil a man's heart."

Kahen: Saher's curse then will be the decisive confrontation. It's either his curse or your conjuration. One's victory is the other's defeat. Get the mirror conjuration ready now and I hope to God that it proves to be more powerful than Saher's curse.

Mushawaz: I hope that my conjuration will resist his magic curse. Come on, Kahen, can you predict what's going to happen?

Kahen began predicting and for that purpose, he sent the eavesdropping devils to listen secretly to the angels.

When the devils returned, they told him what they had heard.

When Kahen heard the news, he was agitated and frightened. Mushawaz asked him: "Why are you so scared? What did the devils tell you?"

Kahen: I hope my prediction is wrong.

Mushawaz: Why? What did you see?

Kahen: The devils were not able to overhear anything. There was a black cloud that prevented them from listening secretly.

Mushawaz: What does that mean, Kahen?

Kahen did not reply. He said to himself, *it means I shall be murdered in this battle. This will be the end for me.*

Kahen: Mushawaz, if I foresee that we are going to lose, we must go to Sumia, Father of the jinn and tell him what we have done and ask him how Saher's magic can be undone.

Mushawaz: Don't worry, my friend. The mirror equation is powerful and effective. I don't think that Saher can undo it.

Kahen: I pray to God for that. Let's prepare the mirror conjuration.

Hence, each one of them started preparing his magic and conjuration. Kahen thought of putting an alternative plan, while also helping Mushawaz with his equations and conjuration. They informed the hidden jinn and devils of their tasks and assignments. Mushawaz said to Kahen: "If we don't overcome Saher, then we must do as I said. One of us goes to Sumia and the other stays here to finish the mirror equation as it requires two foundations to do it. I suggest you go to Sumia and I'll stay here because I was the one who started this hideous act." Kahen agreed although, deep down, there was something else he wanted to do. He hadn't told

125

Mushawaz the truth. The devils had told him that he was going to get killed.

Fearing for Mushawaz's high expectations and state of mind, he did not want to tell him the truth so as not to discourage him. While Mushawaz was busy with his equation, Kahen quickly formed a new one by which he changed and closed the circle of the curse so that it was restricted to the Green City only.

Having finished his equation of changing, Kahen went to Mushawaz and informed him that Saher was waiting for them in the battlefield. Mushawaz said: "Let's go then, everything is ready. My last equation also states that if Saher is defeated, his magic would end and all our books would be burned. The jinn, devils, merdan and ogres would all be released. I have given them our treasures. With that, our work would be finished; our contracts would be void and none of our victims would be harmed anymore."

Meanwhile, Saher was standing in the battlefield with Habel and Nabel. He told them: "Be well- prepared; my curse includes a bet. If we are defeated, the bet would be reversed and we shall all die. But if we win, I shall possess all Kahen and Mushawaz's books and take their devils, soldiers, ogres and merdan, in addition to the sentinels of prediction and conjuration. They will all be mine and I shall become the strongest. Get ready and issue the orders."

Mushawaz and Kahen headed to the battlefield to face Saher, Habel and Nabel.

Saher: I heard that you want to overcome my curse.

Mushawaz: That's right and I shall undo its magic too.

Saher: You will never be able to do that, Mushawaz. The magic of my curse is connected to you and Kahen. I shall do my best to crush you.

Kahen: Saher, I'm going to unravel all Habel and Nabel's riddles.

Habel and Nabel: We shall see how you're going to do that.

They all stood up and began reading incantations and chanting. The force of the magic changed the weather, and Saher's curse began to emerge. The sky was clouded and fog accumulated. The earth cracked. Kahen and Mushawaz sensed the danger and hastened with reading their incantations.

They did not expect the rapid effect of Saher's curse. They were startled by what they saw. Mushawaz was saying to himself, *how could you have come so far, Saher? You have attained the highest levels of magic, which even I, your mentor, could not attain. I considered the idea of the curse impossible to implement. But, oh my God, Have mercy on us!"*

When he was about to end his curse, Saher said to Mushawaz: "Death to my assistants and peace to my enemies."

Kahen: What kind of greeting is that, Mushawaz?

Mushawaz: It's an equation: Death to my assistants and peace to my enemies. Damn him, this is the mirror equation.

Kahen: The mirror? How can he make your own equation? Isn't it supposed to be a secret?

Mushawaz: Yes, but it's similar to the mirror equation. We are his former assistants and his present enemies. Death is the opposite of life.

Kahen: It's clear to me now. By "death to my assistants", he means us; and by "peace to my enemies", he means Habel and Nabel.

Mushawaz: But how can Habel and Nabel be his enemies?

Kahen: This is his curse. It should be interpreted conversely. Try to concentrate a little on this equation. You will find the solution. I broke it up. Look at it:

The magic of the curse maker equals the consent of the three foundations: Saher, Kahen and Mushawaz. Therefore, death, the opposite of life, equals death to the foundations Kahen and Mushawaz. Thus, "my assistants", which is the opposite of "my enemies", is equal to exchanging the foundations, Mushawaz and Kahen, by the new foundations, Habel and Nabel.

Mushawaz: Damn him! How could he have done it so fast? I'm certain that he had planned it before and wanted to replace us with Habel and Nabel in order to continue working without our consent. Hence they become the two new foundations.

Kahen: The devils told me that they overheard that Habel and Nabel have already started the rituals of their riddles.

Mushawaz: Come on, devils, start the mirror conjuration right now. We don't have much time.

All the devils, jinn, merdan and ogres who belonged to the opposing parties started fighting. A fierce battle broke out and many of them died. Each one of them was trying to set up his master's equation. Finally, Mushawaz's soldiers were able to install the mirror equation in the cursed land. Saher felt very weak and told his two assistants: "My God! What has happened to me? I feel so weak now. What is this conjuration?" Habel and Nabel entered the battlefield to see the equation that made Saher so weak, and they discovered the mirror equation which was concealed in the form of riddles. They were enraged because they were the inventors of riddles. Riddles were their own weapon, and Kahen and Mushawaz were confronting them with it.

The riddles were difficult but they were able to solve them. Saher regained his strength. However, as they were solving the riddles, they forgot that there was a conjuration among them. Saher started chanting his last incantation to complete the magic and win the bet. As soon as he said "in the name of God, we have finished", the mirror equation interacted and the magic turned on the magician. Saher didn't notice that change. Habel said to Nabel: "The magic is reversed. We must do something about it. We cannot interrupt Saher's chanting or else we lose the bet. Clearly, Saher hasn't noticed the change. So when he finishes his chanting and incantations, the magic of the curse will reach us and we'll die!" They reflected on an alternative plan and Habel said to Nabel: "Reverse Mushawaz's equation now and let's go down to the location of the riddles that we have solved and find Mushawaz's equation."

They quickly arrived to their destination. Saher was going to finish his chanting any minute. Habel found the equation and said to his brother: "Look here, this is the mirror equation of Mushawaz. By God, we shall die if Saher ceases his chanting. We must undo his equation right now."

They thought of an equation to break the mirror. So they wrote a simple one and began striking the ground with their feet to smash the mirror. They ordered all their soldiers to do the same. The eavesdroppers told Kahen what Habel and Nabel were doing. Kahen knew that he couldn't interrupt Mushawaz's chanting as he and Saher were challenging each other with their incantations. So, he had to go alone with his soldiers to stop the destruction. They arrived there and launched an attack on Habel and Nabel, but the mirror had already been smashed. An eerie silence prevailed in the battlefield.

Mushawaz was unable to move, so he knew that something was wrong. One of the jinn went to him and told him that the mirror had been smashed and Saher's curse was upon them. Seconds later, fires broke out in all quarters of the city. Mushawaz could neither move nor speak. He knew that he had lost and that he was going to die. He looked at his soldiers; they too were unable to move. Saher ordered the killing of these soldiers as a sacrifice to him to increase his power. Habel and Nabel asked him if he wanted to take them as prisoners but he refused. He said: "I don't want any prisoners because I know that if I kill them and sacrifice them in my name, I would become more powerful. Order our soldiers to kill them, and I shall kill Kahen and Mushawaz myself."

Saher went to Mushawaz and spoke to him.

Saher: Do you see, master, that I'm stronger than you?

Mushawaz: Kill me, Saher.

Saher: Do you remember the disappearance equation, the first one you ever taught us?

Mushawaz: What has that got to do with the situation now, Saher? Do you want to make me disappear?

Saher: No, I want to conceal your conjuration to make it look better and stronger.

Saher continued his betting. He read the last of his incantations to conceal his master's conjuration in himself to become stronger. While he was busy reading, Kahen used the exchange equation which made both Kahen and Mushawaz disappear. Mushawaz was surprised by his own disappearance and thought that it was Saher's doing. Kahen took his place, looking exactly like him. He was able to reproduce the shape of the replaced person. When Saher finished his reading, he felt nothing. That surprised him and he thought, *what is this conjuration? Is it possible that I couldn't conceal his*

power? Something wrong has happened! So, I must kill
him now because if stealing his conjuration has failed to
transfer his power to me, then killing him would do it.

Thinking that the person in front of him was Mushawaz,
Saher took his sword and said: " Thank you for teaching
me this science." And he stabbed him in his heart. After
the stabbing, Kahen's exchange equation became void
and ineffective, and he reappeared as his real self. Thus,
Saher acquired the power of prediction but not that of
conjuration.

Saher was shocked and asked Kahen: "Where is
Mushawaz? How did you switch bodies, Kahen? What is
this equation?" But how could Kahen answer him when
he had been stabbed! And that was how the founder of
the science of magic and conjuration, the first father of
prediction, and initiator of the idea of prediction, died.

Saher carried on with his equation and exchanged the
original foundations with the new ones, Habel and Nabel.
However, they were astonished when they found out
that the curse was restricted to the Green City. They
couldn't force their way forward with more curses, as it
was Saher's intention to curse the neighboring cities also.
His curse was trapped due to Kahen's equation which
they couldn't undo because he had died.

After winning both the bet and the battle, Saher killed all
Kahen and Mushawaz's assistants in sacrifice to himself.
Some of the eavesdropping devils were able to escape
and they took Kahen's body with them. Grieving for their
master, they left the Cursed City and went to Sumia,
Father of the jinn, because they knew that Mushawaz
would be there with him. Those were Kahen's last
instructions to them.

When they arrived to the Valley of Worship, they found
Mushawaz with Father Sumia. When the former saw

Kahen's dead body, he couldn't believe his eyes. He cried a lot because he knew that Kahen offered himself as a sacrifice in his place. He asked his servants, "Why did Kahen do that?" and they answered: "When we were eavesdropping, we heard the angels saying that Kahen was going to die. He did not want to tell you that because he was afraid you would lose your enthusiasm and courage."

Father Sumia took Kahen's body to the temple, where it was washed, prayed on and buried.   After that, Mushawaz told Sumia of all that had happened.

In the meantime, Saher didn't realize that he had made a big mistake in the curse equation. He had remembered himself, Habel and Nabel but forgotten to include his soldiers in the equation. Thus they were all cursed and they died right after they had killed the soldiers of Kahen and Mushawaz.   Saher, Habel and Nabel found themselves without the soldiers who served them. To reassemble their forces, they had to start from zero.

Mushawaz pledged to avenge Kahen but not through conjuration this time. He had repented and become a good servant of God. He had changed his name to Shamoun. He knew that Saher was assembling a new army. This time, Shamoun had Sumia, Father of the jinn and the strongest of them, on his side. Everyone feared and respected Sumia. Together, they began to get ready for a confrontation in the near future.

That war took place a very long time ago, long before the era of the Ashkhor Royal Family. It became a legend that was passed from one generation to another.   Some believed it and others didn't.

That was the story of the beginning of the dark ages. Afterwards, the science of magic, conjuration and prediction became famous. To date, their books are still in circulation.

Fifgel: My God! So Saher was the one who made Mared and his comrades disappear. This means that war will break out. Master Fouta, we should leave now and inform King Khorkhis.

Sumia: No, Fifgel. This will remain a secret between us. I suspect that there is a hidden jinni who is watching all our moves. I don't want Saher to notice anything.

Fouta: What should we do then, Sumia?

Sumia: Now is the time for Shamoun's revenge. Go, chamberlain, and tell Shamoun that I want to see him urgently.

Fouta: What do we do now, master Sumia? Will there be war?

Sumia: I see floods of blood covering the earth.

Fifgel: Let's pray to God for mercy. If Saher attacks us with Mared and his comrades, it will be disastrous.

Chamberlain: Master Sumia; Shamoun, the good servant of God, has arrived.

Shamoun: Peace upon the believers in God. What do you want, Father Sumia?

Sumia: And peace upon you too. There is something you must know. We have noticed lately that Saher has started the execution of his plan.

Shamoun: What did he do?

Sumia: He was spotted in the Cursed City. He hid Mared and his comrades' armies somewhere away from the Cursed City. King Khorkhis has declared a state of emergency.

Shamoun: Then the time has come, Father. This means that Saher has prepared his army and he's now stronger than before, after getting his hands on my books and martyr, Kahen's books too.

Sumia: So, Shamoun, let's get our armies ready too and join Khorkhis in his kingdom. We shall fight on his side against Mared and his comrades.

Fifgel: My master, Father Sumia, my time here is up. I apologize to you, but I have to take Wise Fouta back with me now.

Fouta: I'm going with you immediately. Master Sumia, Shamoun, we'll be waiting for you.

Shamoun: Listen to me. You must be very cautious. It is possible that some of the hidden jinn could be present in this palace.

Fifgel: How do we know if they are here?

Shamoun: You cannot. I shall follow you tomorrow and I'll prepare my troops today.

Sumia: Fifgel, go to your king and tell him that Sumia, Father of the jinn, will be on his way tomorrow to support him.

Fifgel: At your command, Father. Let's go, Wise Fouta, King Khorkhis is expecting us.

Fifgel and Wise Fouta went on their way. Fifgel was not the bearer of good news to the king. Nevertheless, the news that would comfort the king was the promised support of Sumia and Shamoun. As soon as they arrived to the kingdom, they found the king in an awful state. They greeted him and when the king saw Fouta, he calmed down a little. Fouta said to him: "Do not fear, your majesty, the Father of the jinn and Shamoun will be here tomorrow to support you in your upcoming war." The king answered, "How are you, Wise Fouta?" and Fouta replied: "I am fine. Forgive me your majesty; I was occupied with God's worship."

Khorkhis: This is your right and you don't have to ask for forgiveness. God's obedience has priority over everything in this world. Fouta, do you remember the dream that I used to have since childhood.

Fouta: You mean the one in which an angel came to you and told you that there would be a ruler other than you?

Khorkhis: Yes, Fouta. I'm still having the same dream although there is a change in it this time.

Fouta: What is the change, your majesty?

Khorkhis: I saw the angels roaming the earth in a strange costume.

Fouta: A strange costume? What did it look like?

Khorkhis: They were standing up as if on alert for war. They had headbands on which was written 'I bear witness that there is no God but Allah'. After having roamed the earth, the writing was transformed into 'accomplished with the grace of God.' What is the meaning of this dream?

Fouta: I swear to God, master, that it is indeed a very strange dream. It's very hard to explain it. I'm no good at interpreting dreams. Tomorrow, Sumia, Father of the jinn, will be here and he'll explain it to you.

Meanwhile, Torn had arrived from the kingdom of the seven jinn. He had good news. He told the king that the jinn had responded and agreed to fight with him against Mared and his comrades. They were also getting their armies ready. He was followed by Darl who told the king that he had bad news for him.

Darl: Your majesty, I have bad news for you.

Khorkhis: What is it, Darl? Speak.

Darl: The devils refused to back us up. King Sharaeel said he was siding with Saher.

Khorkhis: Saher! How could King Sharaeel say that? How could he believe in the legend of Saher!?

Darl: That was what Sharaeel told me. The other kings—
Asater, Anafeer, Zaiboun and Rakhel—all agreed with
him.

Khorkhis: Damn them all! How can Sharaeel betray us
after signing the pact? Didn't you tell him that he had
already pledged allegiance?

Darl: I did. But his reply was that the devils will stand
against you and that they will get Khaji back on their side
as their ally.

Khorkhis: So we have lost the devils.

Darl: Why do you care so much for them? They are
helpless without the Great Black Devils Army
commanded by Khaji.

Khorkhis: Darl, you know that Khaji is one of the devils,
and he will not back us up against his own people. You
don't know the devils. I'm sure that Khaji will stand
against us and he will be the reason for our defeat if he
stays amongst us. If his Black Army attacks our city, the
situation will be reversed.

Darl: Your majesty, how can you doubt Khaji's loyalty?
He has been with you since the reign of your father, King
Khafan. He has never betrayed your royal family. Why
would he do so now?

Khorkhis: The situation is different now. During my
father's reign, the devils never betrayed him.

Fouta: Master, it is wise under the circumstances to
amass the greatest number of troops. You will be
confronting Mared, Markhof and Sourfag, in addition to
Saher.

Khorkhis: Even you, Fouta, believe in Saher's existence?

Fouta: Yes sir. He does exist.

Hence, Wise Fouta was forced to recount Saher's story
to King Khorkhis. If he didn't do so, Khorkhis would
dismiss Khaji. He felt compelled to warn the king about

136

the force he was going to face. Khorkhis was convinced of the truth of the wise man's words but still insisted on his decision. He told his chamberlain Bilban:

"You will forbid Khaji and Sural from entering. I am certain that these two are responsible for the treason."

Fouta: What are you doing, your majesty? Are you dismissing two of your best commanders?

Khorkhis: Indeed I am when they betray their king.

Fouta: But they didn't betray you!

Khorkhis: How could they not have betrayed me when Khaji's own devils did? He's one of them. The devils had offered Khaji and his soldiers as a gift to my father, King Khafan, and now they are betraying me.

Fouta: What are you talking about, sir? What's that got to do with getting rid of Khaji?

Khorkhis: And I shall dispense with Sural too! One of my secret soldiers told me that he was whispering in Khaji's ear on the Day of Allegiance. He told Khaji that he was seeing a lot of blood but I didn't believe the soldier at the time. However, when I had the chance, I sent Khaji and Sural to the Forbidden City and I told myself that if they said they didn't find Mared and his comrades, it meant that it was all a premeditated plot. What I suspected did happen. So now I shall forbid them from entering the kingdom. I shall even murder them at the gates!

Fouta: Calm down, your majesty. The war is forcing you to make rash decisions.

Khorkhis: I have made up my mind. Bilban, go to the guards at the gates and pick out the two most skilled in aiming. Tell them to aim one arrow at Khaji's heart and another at Sural's heart. Tell them that if they succeed in this mission, they will replace Khaji and Sural.

137

Fouta: Please don't make a reckless decision. If we lose Khaji and Sural, Mared would have a much bigger opportunity of destroying the kingdom.

Khorkhis: I have my secret guards and they are enough for me. I don't need these two traitors. Go Bilban, and issue the orders without delay. Get out of here, all of you. I wish to pray to God and ask for His guidance!

Sad and disappointed, Bilban, Fouta and the commanders left the king alone. Fouta said out loud: "You were right, Khafan, when you told me that this son of yours was reckless and unsuited for a king's position."

Bilban: Forget that now, Fouta. What shall I do? Should I execute the king's orders? If I don't and he knows about it, he would surely kill me. As you can see, he is reckless. How can he dispense with Khaji and Sural so easily? By God, something strange is going on!

Fifgel: Listen, Bilban, go and tell the guards, and I shall fly to Khaji and Sural to inform them of what has happened so that they do not return to the kingdom.

Torn: Fifgel, if they do not return, the king will be suspicious.

Fouta: Let him go, Torn. The king is already suspecting them of treason; in fact, he is certain of it.

Fifgel then proceeded to warn Khaji and Sural, and Bilban went to issue the king's commands to the guards. Two of the guards, Charle and Sirakh, were chosen to execute the king's orders. They were surprised by the king's decision, but when they saw his stamp, they agreed. Bilban told them: "The king wants you to know that if you kill Khaji and Sural, he will reward you by appointing you as the new commanders in their places." They were greatly pleased with that decision, as the commander's position was an extremely important one. Highly excited, they started getting ready for their mission.

The Kingdom of the Devils

After their coup against King Khorkhis, the devils were on high alert. They were afraid because they had taken a quick and impulsive decision. King Sharaeel was behind that decision, as he was sure that Mared and his comrades were going to support him. Mared's message to him on the day of Allegiance made him take that decision. Moreover, after they had found out about the escape of Mared and his comrades from the Forbidden City, with the help of Saher, they had felt more proud and powerful. They were hoping to receive news from Mared any minute.

King Asater: And now, Sharaeel, we have revolted against Khorkhis and betrayed him. What if Mared betrays us and doesn't keep his promise?

Sharaeel: He will keep his promise. After his escape, Mared will come to us seeking the support of our armies.

King Rakhel: You all know that Saher is also with him. He won't need us.

King Zaiboun: I swear I still remember when Saher came to our forefathers and we were then our fathers' successors. He introduced himself as well as Habel and Nabel.

King Anafeer: And my father, King Ankhouran, said that Saher was a madman.

King Sharaeel: No, he is not mad. We all know the story of the curse. If Kahen's devils had not come to us and

139

told us that story, we would have remained as ignorant as the rest of the jinn.

King Asater: Is any of Kahen's devils still alive?

King Sharaeel: There's only one by the name of Saraheel. The rest of them were affected by the curse.

The devils ordered their servants to summon Saraheel immediately. They knew that Kahen had been able to predict future events through eavesdropping. Saraheel was one of his close pupils. They wanted him to predict their future. Saraheel arrived and greeted the five kings of the devils: "Peace upon you, kings of the devils. Why did you summon me?"

King Sharaeel: And peace upon you too, Saraheel. You're so much older now. I wouldn't have recognized you if you hadn't introduced yourself.

Saraheel: This is due to Saher's curse. I suffer from it daily. I'm weak and I feel death approaching.

King Anafeer: We need something from you.

Saraheel: I know. You want me to predict for you.

King Zaiboun: How did you know that? Did you predict that we were going to need your help before coming here?

Saraheel: Yes indeed. And it is the power of prediction that is helping my body resist Saher's curse.

King Rakhel: Then can you tell us, Saraheel, if Mared is coming to us or not?

Saraheel was silent for a while. He began reciting the prediction incantations. After he finished, he said: "I can't see anything. Damn him! Saher has formed an equation so that no one can predict this event."

King Asater: This means that Saher is with Mared. What do you want us to do now, Sharaeel?

King Sharaeel: We should wait for three days. If we don't have any news from Mared or Saher, we must confront

King Khorkhis. We have no other choice because we have taken a tough decision. If Mared betrays us, Khorkhis will attack us. We don't want that to happen, so we shall attack him first. Inform your commanders of this decision so they would get ready and well equipped.

King Anafeer: I shall dispatch one of my devils to track Mared and Saher and tell them that we are on their side.

King Asater: I shall send one of my spies to check out what's happening in the kingdom of the seven jinn. They are our old enemies and we must know what they're up to.

King Zaiboun: And I shall send someone to Khorkhis' kingdom to see what's happening there after we broke our pledge.

Saraheel: My master, King Sharaeel, I have just received news from the eavesdroppers.

King Sharaeel: And what did they tell you?

Saraheel: That Khorkhis has let go of Khaji and Sural and accused them of treason.

King Rakhel: Treason! Is that possible? What did they do to make him dispense with the Black and Red Armies?

Saraheel: He thought that they had liberated Mared and his comrades from the Forbidden City.

King Sharaeel: This is good news! Without the Black and Red Armies, Khorkhis will suffer an utter defeat.

King Rakhel: At last Khaji will come back to us with his army. We shall be stronger than Mared and Khorkhis.

King Sharaeel: Don't be overjoyed. Nothing has happened yet. Let's wait for the return of Khaji.

The Kingdom of the Seven Jinn

The news of Mared's escape from the Forbidden City and the fleeing of the soldiers who guarded it spread like fire. People were very scared and especially when they heard about the unprecedented massacre. The city was in a state of terror and rumors spread. The seven kings of the jinn tried to allay the common people's fears by telling them that Khorkhis was going to crush Mared and his comrades before they reached their kingdom They told them not to forget that they were strong and that Khorkhis had the best six commanders. The kings of the jinn were not aware of what had happened to the six commanders and the latest developments in the kingdom. They thought that King Khorkhis was preparing the armies and that his messenger would arrive any minute to order them to move to the battlefront.

Queen Houran: The troops are ready for the confrontation, and the city is on alert.

Queen Tuyour: Yes. We must be on alert. Our enemy is tough.

The jinn started organizing their ranks. They were renowned for their strength and intelligence. As soon as they started the organization process, the military parade began. It was a frightening but beautiful sight. Each one of the kings and queens had his/her own special army. Queen Houran's soldiers stood out with their beauty and supreme force. Queen Tuyour's soldiers were excellent flyers, while King Saleh's soldiers were characterized by their wisdom. King Ahmar's soldiers, including Sural who was one of the six commanders that served King Khorkhis, stood out with their great speed. King Aswad's soldiers equaled Khaji's soldiers in strength, although the former were of the jinn and the latter of the devils. Also parading were King Katel's soldiers. King Katel was given that name because his soldiers were known for their spying, treachery and killing.

As for Queen Sheikha, her army was reputed for accomplishing difficult missions. They were the jinn of the desert and were able to tolerate the harshest conditions.

The parade started and it proved to be a powerful one. Everyone was feeling proud of himself and his power. The seven kings later entered the secret room to discuss the impending war. The chamberlain of Queen Sheikha followed them and announced that commanders Fifgel and Sural were asking for permission to enter. Queen Sheikha was astonished. She addressed the other kings: "Fifgel and Sural! Shouldn't there be one commander only?" Queen Tuyour replied: "There must be something wrong! Why would Khorkhis send Fifgel and Sural? Why didn't his messenger come?" After some deliberation, Queen Sheikha gave her permission for Fifgel and Sural to see her and ordered the chamberlain to let them in the secret room.

The two commanders entered. Sural looked shocked and Fifgel looked disappointed. The kings were startled by their looks, and Queen Sheikha asked: "What's wrong, commanders? Aren't you supposed to be at the battlefront now?"

Sural: I have been released from my position and the king wants me dead.

Queen Tuyour: What? Is that true?

143

King Katel: But why, Sural? Have you betrayed King Khorkhis in any way?

Fifgel: I swear by God that he hasn't. King Khorkhis has lost his mind.

That was when Fifgel told them the whole story.

King Saleh: My God! How could Khorkhis do that? What has hit him?

King Ahmar: Don't be afraid, Sural. We are here with you. King Khorkhis cannot kill you.

King Aswad: What did Khaji say when he knew that the king wanted him dead too?

Fifgel: At first, Khaji didn't believe me. He thought I was mad. He continued on his way to the kingdom, albeit very cautiously. As he approached the gate, arrows started flying at him from all directions. He escaped and our paths crossed. He admitted to me that what I had told him was coming true. So I told him that something weird was going on and that Khorkhis was not the king that we knew. Khaji declared that he had no country to go back to and that he had only one land; the land of the devils. I told him that the devils had decided to antagonize King Khorkhis and I asked him what he intended to do. He replied that he was forced to be on their side, but that if we ever happened to meet in the battlefield, I should keep out of his way so that we would not be forced to fight each other. Then Khaji headed for the kingdom of the devils.

King Saleh: What are you saying? The kings of the devils have broken their pledge to Khorkhis?

Fifgel: Yes, and they declared their support to Mared and Saher.

Queen Sheikha: So the devils believe in Saher's existence. And they side with Mared and Saher against us.

Queen Tuyour: Whom do you mean by Saher, Sheikha? Is it the same Saher who cast his curse on the Green City?

Queen Houran: But isn't Saher dead, King Saleh? Do you remember the time when we sent some of our soldiers on a secret mission to kill Saher? The soldiers told us that the Cursed City was deserted and that when they asked some people about Saher, they were told that he had died.

King Katel: True, that's what they said. But I see now that Saher is still alive. He is behind the escape of Mared and his comrades. What shall we do now? King Khorkhis has lost two of his commanders and only four are left.

Queen Sheikha: Then our enemies at the moment are Mared, Markhof, Sourfag, Saher, Habel and Nabel; in addition to the five kings of the devils and Khaji. God, what a mighty army!

King Ahmar: I shall withdraw from this battle.

King Aswad: And so shall I.

King Saleh: What's the matter with you two? How can you do that? Are you afraid of Mared and Saher that much?

King Ahmar: No, I'm not afraid. But what's the use of fighting for a king who might kill me or dismiss me after the victory? King Khorkhis has ordered the killing of Sural disregarding his position as one of my best commanders and favorite soldiers. Will he even care if we fight with him or against him?

Queen Houran: But you know, Ahmar, that if we do not all join forces with King Khorkhis, our entire world would be destroyed. Do you want Saher to carry his curse through and destroy all our countries?

King Ahmar: King Khorkhis has betrayed us and ordered the killing of Sural. This is unacceptable and he should be made to regret this act.

Queen Sheikha: Calm down, all of you. Hatred and quarreling are useless. Be calm, Ahmar and Aswad. We must all stand united or else we'll all be killed. Remember that the devils have been our enemies from the beginning of time. They will have no mercy on us. They could slaughter everyone in our kingdom when they get the chance. We, the kings and queens, must not allow that to happen.

King Aswad: I have made up my mind and I'm not going to change it. I'm not leading my army in a battle under that stupid king's banner.

King Saleh: Alright then. You stay here and protect the city. Don't leave it.

King Ahmar: We shall stay here, but without your instructions. If we want to go out, we shall.

Queen Sheikha: Please stay calm, everybody. Fifgel, go to King Khorkhis right now before he has reason to doubt you.

Fifgel: Don't worry, your majesties, we have Father Sumia and Mushawaz on our side.

King Saleh: The Father of the Jinn will join us in this war! Thank God for that! This is indeed great power.

Fifgel left the palace of the kings of the jinn bearing with him so much bad news. King Aswad and King Ahmar withdrew from the battle. The situation was deteriorating day after day. They had lost the support of two of the kings, Kings Aswad and Ahmar, and two commanders, Khaji and Sural. Fifgel hoped that the war would soon start before any more kings and commanders refused to fight in it.

After Fifgel's exit from the palace of the kings of the jinn, King Khorkhis' messenger arrived and told them: "King Khorkhis commands you to proceed to him with your armies at once." Queen Houran replied: "Go to your king

146

and tell him we shall go to him immediately; as soon as we finish our preparations."

The messenger returned to the kingdom of Khorkhis after obtaining the pledge of the kings of the jinn.

Queen Houran: King Aswad, King Ahmar, do you want to come with us or do you insist on staying here?

King Ahmar: Queen Houran, I have already given you my answer and I'm not going back on my words.

King Aswad: And me neither, Queen Houran. King Khorkhis' conduct has angered me. He's not worthy of my protection of him and subsequently losing my soldiers.

King Saleh: Let's move then, Houran. We don't have much time. King Khorkhis is waiting for us.

Queen Sheikha: What shall we tell Khorkhis if he asks us about Ahmar and Aswad?

Queen Tuyour: We tell him that we have left them behind to protect our kingdom. We cannot leave our people defenseless.

Queen Houran: Yes, that's what we shall say. But I do hope, King Aswad and King Ahmar, that you would go back on your decision. Anger is not going to help our situation. It is wise that we all stand as one. When we are done with this disaster, you can do what you want.

The five kings went out, leaving the two kings, Aswad and Ahmar, behind. They left, feeling uncertain of their victory because their leader this time was not the clever Khafan, but the reckless Khorkhis. They prayed to God to protect them from the evil of Mared and Saher.

The Kingdom of Khorkhis

Father Sumia and Mushawaz arrived to the kingdom where they were warmly greeted. Sumia was very much loved by his people; he was their father and the first of the jinn population born in the world. He had his own special status and strength. His good soldiers accompanied him on that trip. Khorkhis received him with the respect due to his status and declared: "God Bless you, Father. We are blessed by your coming here to support us."

Father Sumia was much-fatigued by his journey. The Valley of Worship was very far from the kingdom of Khorkhis. He went to take a rest in his room in the palace. As soon as he immersed his feet in hot water, Wise Fouta entered his room in a hurry as if he wanted to relay something very important to him.

Fouta: My master, Father Sumia, bless you. There is something you must know.

Sumia: What's the matter, Fouta?

Fouta: Things have happened that you must be aware of.

Sumia: What has happened?

Fouta: Commanders Khaji and Sural have been dispensed with. Moreover, commander Fifgel told me, after his arrival from the kingdom of the jinn, that the two kings Ahmar and Aswad were upset by Khorkhis' action and they refused to join him in the fighting. As you know, Sural belongs to King Ahmar's community. Khaji is a cousin of King Aswad's who is partly jinn and partly devil.

Khaji has joined forces with the devils that are going to fight against us.

Sumia: What's going on here? Why did Khorkhis act so recklessly?

Fouta: I swear to you, master, that Khorkhis has become erratic. How could he have done that? Even young boys do not behave the way he did. I don't know... sometimes I see that he has the brains of a king and other times I see that he has the brains of a child. Something weird is happening to him!

Sumia: Go to my assistant Shamoun, and tell him to come immediately.

Fouta: Sir, there's something more serious still.

Sumia: You will tell me about it when you bring Shamoun.

Fouta left. He decided to tell Sumia everything that was on his mind in case the latter had a different opinion. He reached Shamoun's room and informed him that Sumia wanted to see him at once.

Shamoun sensed an emergency at hand. He went hurriedly with Fouta and asked his master if something was wrong.

Sumia: Fouta wants to say something and I wanted you to be present. What did you want to say, Fouta?

Fouta: Sir, King Khorkhis told me about a frightful dream that he had had and I didn't explain it to him.

Sumia: What was the dream, Fouta?

Fouta: King Khorkhis dreamed that the angels were roaming the earth dressed as warriors. They had headbands on which was written 'There's no God but Allah'. After roaming the earth, those words were replaced by other words, 'accomplished with the grace of God'. Then one of the angels went to him and told him, "God will appoint a ruler over Earth, other than the jinn."

Sumia: My God! What is this dream? How did you explain it, Fouta?

Fouta: Sir, this means the end of our era. It means that God will wreak his wrath upon us!

Sumia: That's right. This is how I would interpret it too.

Shamoun: What shall we do now?

Sumia: I shall pray to God to have mercy on us all and not bring down his wrath upon us. If God gets angry with us, we lose everything.

Fouta: I do hope that our interpretation of the dream is incorrect.

Sumia: I hope so, Fouta, although it's highly probable that it's going to happen. But we shall pray to God as much as we can. Shamoun, I also requested your presence because I have reached a strange conclusion. I need your advice.

Shamoun: Yes sir. What is it you wanted?

Sumia: Do you remember when you told me that Saher tried to make some jinn get into the bodies of other jinn in order to control them?

Shamoun: Yes, I do. But that was one of Saher's dreams. We both tried to find the appropriate equation for it but we failed.

Sumia: And what else did you tell me, Shamoun? Do you remember saying to me that if Saher succeeded in forming this equation, he would be able to control the person?

Shamoun: There are other things too. If Saher succeeds in letting a jinni enter the body of another, he can cause the latter very strange and fatal diseases. He can affect his active brain too and transform it into a passive brain with the help of the brain-changing equation. That was written in his books, but we never put it into practice because we didn't have the complete information. As you know, the science of conjuration, magic and prediction depends also on the stars and astronomy and the element of the person. To complete this equation, Saher must first master all the equations.

Sumia: Are you able to tell if a person is affected by this kind of magic?

Shamoun: Who is the person in question?

Sumia: I'm talking about King Khorkhis.

Shamoun: What? Do you mean that King Khorkhis is possessed by this kind of magic? Why did you suspect him?

Sumia: His recent behavior has made me feel that he was under a magic spell. Fouta, go to King Khorkhis at once and tell him that Father Sumia and Shamoun request an audience with him. Go now, I need to discuss something with Shamoun.

Fouta did as he was told. The king agreed, saying that he could not refuse Father Sumia's request. Sumia could visit him any time he wanted. He sent one of his servants to bring them. Khorkhis didn't know what awaited him in that simple visit. Sumia and Shamoun wanted to confirm whether Saher had completed the equation or not.

Sumia: What are you going to do now, Shamoun?

Shamoun: Father, we were the initiators of these equations. The first one we ever did was linked to religion. It entailed slaughtering for the sake of someone other than God even if the rituals remained the same. So, we reverse the equation and confront Saher's magic this time with religion. The only flaw in the equation of the jinn's entry into other bodies was that the intruding jinn would become weak. The only equation that would force them to leave the bodies, or to speak, was

151

mentioning God's name over the patient's body. Those were mere assumptions that were not implemented.

Sumia: How can mentioning God's name force them to come out?

Shamoun: Because we started the first magic equation by mentioning God and slaughtering for another. This is the basis of magic, conjuration and prediction. If we reverse it, then slaughtering for God would reverse the magic or conjuration. So the jinn would either speak or leave the body.

Sumia: My God! What kind of knowledge have you acquired, Shamoun!

Shamoun: I know, master, and I ask God to forgive me. I shall do my utmost to stop Saher. But sir, there is something that must be done first.

Sumia: What is it, Shamoun?

Shamoun: If I want to find out if Khorkhis is under a magic spell, I must rename myself Mushawaz to complete the equation. All the equations are linked to my name.

Sumia: So be it. Let's go to King Khorkhis now.

Shamoun: Before we go, I shall recite the praises of God over this water, and the king should drink it. Then we'll see what happens. If my assumptions are right, the hidden jinni will appear.

Sumia: Get on with it. The king is waiting for us.

Shamoun recited the praises of God over the water and puffed in it. Then they went to King Khorkhis. He was in his private chamber with Bilban and Fouta. The king addressed them: "What's the matter, God's good worshippers? Why did you come to me at this time? It must be something urgent that is related to the war."

Sumia replied: "It is indeed, your majesty. The situation at present has become very serious and we must talk.

But first, please drink this water from the holy Valley of Worship."

Khorkhis drank the water and as soon as he finished drinking, his features started to change. His voice started changing too and he looked and sounded like someone else; someone they did not recognize. He spoke in a hoarse mocking voice: "You have discovered the truth, Mushawaz. You solved the equation. You are still as smart as before."

Mushawaz: So Saher succeeded in his body-entering equation.

Sumia: You cursed jinni! What is your name and to which branch of jinn do you belong?

The jinni: My name is Thabeel and I'm from the merdan. If anyone else had asked me this question, Father, I wouldn't have given him an answer.

Mushawaz: Thabeel, I order you to leave this body.

Thabeel: You know, Mushawaz, that if I leave Khorkhis' body, I would die.

Mushawaz: Then tell me which type of magic this is, Thabeel, and what is your mission?

Thabeel: Each magic has its contract in which the type of magic is inscribed. It must be executed. You know that very well, Mushawaz, and you know that if I don't go through with it, the sentinels of magic would kill me.

Mushawaz: Give me the text of the contract now, Thabeel, and go in peace. I shall exchange the killing text with the peace text and put my stamp on it. The sentinels will not come near you because I shall hide you so that they won't be able to see you. If you refuse to go, I shall kill you myself, and you know that I can do it. Don't forget that it was I who established this science.

153

Thabeel: I know you very well, Mushawaz. I shall come out, but don't forget your promise to me. Here is the contract.

Mushawaz took the contract and read it in front of everyone present. They were all startled by its content which read the following:

"Fire to my assistants and peace to my enemies,

All creatures in heaven and earth, praise God and worship Him...

Allah is my God and I'm his slave. To you, my God, I offer my sacrifice...

The fly is slaughtered in my name, the sheep is slaughtered for my work, the jinni is slaughtered in my name and the demon is slaughtered for my magic. My curse struck your city and it will strike all my enemies. With you, the Ashkhor family, I start, and with you, Houran, I connect, and with you, Khafan's brothers, I end. I offer Khafan's children in sacrifice.

You, Sural, are my scapegoat; and you, Khaji, are my victory. I curse you many times. Death to all of you! Blood from the Ashkhor family will pour over Houran and would be drunk by Khaji and Sural. I raise my banner with you Mared, and I increase my power with your comrades Sourfag and Markhof. The moon rises and sets, the sun rises and sets. I write my contract with you, Mared and comrades. With peace to my enemies I end. May everyone whose name I mentioned, die. He, who doesn't die, will be struck by ignorance and idiocy. The body-entering equation equals the mirage in the desert which means the death of anyone who tries to pursue it—which is the same as the quicksand and equal to the bodies of the Ashkhor dynasty and Khaji and Sural and Houran. Therefore, the body swallows the jinn and the curse is implanted in it."

154

Mushawaz: My God! What is this equation? Saher has become more powerful and knowledgeable than ever before.

Sumia: What does it mean, Mushawaz? The words are unintelligible and ambiguous.

Mushawaz: These are the chants of magic. This is one of his curses and it is called The Curse of Death. In the past, we thought that it was impossible to make a jinni enter into a body. We used to say that we should come up with a very strong equation. Any mistake and that jinni would die. I didn't know that Saher had mastered it because the chants of this magic are very complicated. Saher has done everything conversely. He mentioned God's name and the sacrifice in His name, but he slaughtered in his own name. That is an equation. Then he mentioned the cursed persons, and this is a part of the curse's magic. Later on, he explained that according to the contract, he was going to destroy the Ashkhor dynasty by fatal diseases. That's what he meant when he said, "The demon is slaughtered by my magic." The Ashkhors are demons. Then he said that Queen Houran is a connection, which means that she is a basis. Later, he mentioned Khaji and Sural. The scapegoat, which is Sural, should be slaughtered and Khaji would be victorious after joining forces with the devils. Thus the curse would be complete. When he said that the blood of the Ashkhor family would pour over Sural and Khaji, he meant that Sural and Khaji's war would cause bloodshed in the kingdom and the reason was a member of the Ashkhor Family. He completed the equation of the jinn's entrance into the body by mentioning the mirage; an illusion which we mistake for water in the desert. Also quicksand is known for swallowing anyone who stands in it. He compared it to the body so that the jinni could enter the body and with that, Saher completed the body-entering equation.

Fouta: You mean that this magic was the reason of the disease that struck the Ashkhor family and the cause of their death?

Mushawaz: Yes. That is the reason for their illness and their death. It was Saher's doing.

Sumia: But why didn't Khorkhis die? And why does he mention Houran and not the rest of the kings of the jinn?

Mushawaz: Saher wanted Khorkhis to live so that he could use him to cause disorder and unrest. The equation and the chants are ambiguous because they contain the riddles of Habel and Nabel. Thank God, I have solved it and no one would be able to understand their riddles except myself and Kahen. Saher also wanted to keep Khorkhis alive because his star is the air star, which is easy to control. That way, their plan would work out. The star of the rest of his family—his uncles and brothers and even his father, Khafan—was the earth star. People with the earth star are not easy to control. Only a curse and the magic of death can finish them. Choosing Houran is evidence of the wickedness of Saher. At the time when I worked with Kahen and Saher, we discovered that if we put a spell on a person using his mother's name and put a spell on his mother too, the magic spell would be stronger. The mother carried the baby in her womb and she made sure that it would come to no harm. She endured all discomfort in order to deliver a healthy child. Inside his mother's womb, a baby is protected from all external conditions. We all know that Khafan married Princess Sanaheb, daughter of King Rah, and they had a child, Khorkhis. Sanaheb is the elder sister of Houran who later became queen. After the death of Sanaheb by the same disease that struck her husband Khafan, Saher was forced to find a replacement and Houran was that replacement because she had the same blood as her sister Sanaheb. Anything that afflicted Khorkhis would afflict Houran too. However, Khorkhis would not be affected but Houran, the affectionate mother, would.

Sumia: This means that Saher was behind all Khorkhis' decisions about Sural and Khaji. And Houran is bewitched too!

Fouta: Do you mean, Mushawaz, that Khorkhis' idiotic behavior was not intentional?

Mushawaz: Yes, he is bewitched. A bewitched person does things unwillingly. He cannot control his actions. When the jinni inside him appears to him, the person loses consciousness. So the jinni inside the possessed person does stupid things and takes crucial decisions, as Thabeel did, like dispensing with Khaji and Sural, for example. When the person regains consciousness, he doesn't remember what happened to him.

Thabeel: You are right, Mushawaz, about everything you said. But Saher made a mistake that he could not rectify.

Mushawaz: What was that mistake?

Thabeel: Queen Houran had a maid-in-waiting called the nymph, whose star was the same as that of Houran's. She was her chief maid-in-waiting and she accompanied the queen wherever she went. Sometimes she was also called Houran. In his equation, Saher did not specify which one of them he meant, and there were two of them with the same name and star. When Saher started working his magic and we entered the bodies, the jinni who was supposed to enter Queen Houran's body made a mistake and entered the nymph's body instead. He didn't know it and he thought she was the intended person. The purpose was to make Houran endure anything that befell Khorkhis so that he wouldn't get sick. A female's body is used to pain because it endures pregnancy and childbirth. So when Saher ordered the jinni in charge of Houran to take her to the Cursed City in order to put his imprint on her, he discovered the jinni's mistake. He told him: "Take this maid back and correct your mistake, or else you will die." The jinni, who was one of the small jinn, was afraid. Upon his return to the kingdom, he didn't know what to do, so he made a stupid decision and said that he had seen a child in the Cursed City and

that some sea beasts had tried to kill him. He was sent back there with two soldiers, Harek and Sahek. He hadn't expected that to happen. He only wanted to correct his mistake and get into Houran's body. However, to do that, he had to repeat the equation from the start, which was very hard for him to do. He said to himself, *I shall send these two soldiers to Saher, and he will forgive me because they are two of the best soldiers.* When he arrived to the Cursed City, Habel and Nabel had already told Saher what the small jinni had done. Saher was outraged and told them to leave him alone and to let Harek and Sahek do what they wanted with him. Habel and Nabel then asked two of the servants of magic to wear the costume of Mared's soldiers. They ordered them to go to the jinni in charge of the nymph's body and tell him that Saher no longer needed his services. When they told him that, the jinni got furious and he killed the bird which brought them to him. Harek and Sahek were watching him from above and that was when they attacked and killed one of the servants and captured the other. They also took the nymph to stand trial. The jinn all thought that the nymph had betrayed them but in reality, it wasn't the nymph who was speaking but the jinni inside her. So she was killed along with him and the captured servant.

Mushawaz: So now one of the pillars of his magic is shaken because of the nymph.

Thabeel: Yes, and that's why he decided to change the equation.

Mushawaz: What? Change it? Where did he put the replacement?

Thabeel: I don't know. He put a replacement and that replacement has become the basis instead of me.

Mushawaz: So even if we undo this magic, there's a replacement for it. I wonder where he put the replacement. Tell me, Thabeel, what is this replacement? Is it another contract?

Thabeel: Yes it is. It's a contract that summarizes the curse contract, and it's emplaced in the replacement. This means that he is the one who controls the curse now.

Sumia: What is it, Mushawaz? What do you mean by replacement?

Mushawaz: The replacement means the basis of all the bases, that is, if the magic in Khorkhis is undone now, its effect would remain. In a magic equation, if one of the provisions is imbalanced, the magic is gone. In this case, one of the provisions, which is the death of the connection, the nymph, is gone. Thus the magic should have lost its effect because one of the bases is gone. However, a replacement means a support. No matter how many provisions or bases are gone, the magic remains. The replacement has a very important task. If the magic fails and all the bases die, the holder of the replacement dies. This is a very complicated method and I think it's the first time that Saher uses it.

Thabeel: Indeed, it is the first of its kind. But we still don't know where he put the replacement.

Mushawaz: Thabeel, here is the text of the contract. I'm changing it to a peace contract and taking you out of the body. Go in peace with your assistants because I have exchanged the text of your killing with the disappearance equation. The sentinels and servants of magic will not see you.

Thabeel: Bless you, Mushawaz. But I have no country to go to. As you know, I was forced to do this to get my reward. Now that I've lost it, please accept me as one of your soldiers. I shall be very useful to you in undoing acts of magic.

Mushawaz: You got what you wanted.

Thabeel left the king's body and so did all his assistants who were there with him to help him complete the magic. King Khorkhis lost consciousness and came to after one hour. He saw Mushawaz, Father Sumia, Fouta and Bilban watching him and talking to him. Khorkhis was surprised at the presence of Sumia and asked him how long he had been in the kingdom. They realized that he had been unconscious. Thabeel said: "He has been unconscious ever since Mared left the Forbidden City."

They told Khorkhis about all the events that had occurred, and he couldn't believe what he heard. They told him that he had been under Saher's magic spell and about the decisions that he had taken while under that spell. Khorkhis was shocked and outraged. He declared his intention to go to the kingdom of the devils and teach them a lesson they would never forget.

Sumia: My son, you have already lost two of your best commanders. Do you think that now is the right time for fighting the devils?

Bilban: The kings cf the jinn have arrived with their armies.

Khorkhis: Let the kings in now. I want to talk to them.

The kings of the jinn entered, but there were only five of them, not seven. Khorkhis was informed of the reason for the absence of Kings Ahmar and Aswad. Khorkhis, who had already regained his consciousness after getting back his old self, addressed the kings of the jinn:

"Peace upon the believers in only one God,

I swear to God that I sincerely apologize for my foolhardiness and for any reckless decision that I made. Only God knows that I was not responsible for my actions. It was Saher's magic that reduced me to a child who couldn't control his feelings and who took imprudent decisions. But thank God my magic is now undone and I have returned to my senses. I tell you now that I shall make amendments for everything. I know that kings Ahmar and Aswad refused to join you after I dismissed Sural and Khaji at the time when I was bewitched."

Queen Houran: First of all, peace upon you all and peace upon Father Sumia. Your majesty, what are you talking about? Were you under one of Saher's magic spells?

Sumia: And peace upon you my sons, kings of the jinn. Yes, everything that Khorkhis said is true.

Sumia recounted al the past events and the kings were greatly shocked. They declared that if a war broke out, it was going to be very tough on them with the existence of Saher's magic. Khorkhis told them that he would first crush the traitors, the kings of the devils, and show them the real power of the demons. He had had enough of their ridiculing him.

The Ashkhor dynasty was a descendant of the demons branch, which was one of the rarest branches. They were not numerous. With time, the demons were united and became known as the Ashkhor family. Their power enabled them to unify the whole country. The demons were different from the rest of the jinn branches. When they were furious and had to go to war, they transformed themselves into strong, horrifying shapes. That was their other face.

King Khorkhis sounded his bugle and the entire army of secret royal forces assembled. They were all demons. They gathered in one line and started their transformation. It was a frightening sight that made everyone sense the power of King Khorkhis. This time, they all looked up to him as the king in command.

When Khorkhis finished changing, he looked as grand as a king should look. He became taller, stronger in build and his features seemed fiercer. After the change, a demon would also be able to fly.

Bilban went to him, put the crown on his head and dressed him in the royal military costume. In a thunderous voice, Khorkhis shouted: "I shall kill every traitor who stood in my way. I shall bring peace back to my country. Stay here, kings. I'm going to pay the kings of the devils a short visit."

Furious, Khorkhis left his palace along with his army of changing demons. They flew to the kingdom of devils, carrying with them the weapons of fury.

Sumia: May God be with you, my son. I swear to God that it is very painful for me to see my children fighting and shedding blood.

Queen Houran: My God! I have heard about the changing of demons but I never expected to see Khorkhis looking so magnificent.   Forgive me, my nymph, I have wrongfully murdered you.

The Kingdom of the Devils

Saher's messenger arrived to the kingdom of the devils with a note from Saher and Mared. He addressed them: "Fire to my supporters and peace to my enemies." The devils replied, "And peace upon our leader."

Messenger: Mared told us that he had sent you a letter with King Sharaeel on the day of Allegiance. I have come to you, kings of the devils, to know your answer to that letter.

King Sharaeel: On behalf of all the kings, I'm informing you that we shall all join forces with Saher, Mared and his comrades.

Messenger: This means that you consent to pay allegiance to Saher and Mared now. This is the agreement of allegiance to Saher. Seal it with your stamps and your blood as well.

The allegiance parchment was incomprehensible. It contained many charts, lists and scattered letters which the devils did not understand. But what was the use of questioning it now? If they did not join forces with Mared, they would be attacked by the two opposing parties. The devils sealed the parchment with their stamps and their blood without comprehending the text of the parchment. They were also surprised by the idea of sealing with blood, but they did not ask the messenger for the reason.

Messenger: You, five kings of the devils, have agreed to obey Saher whatever his commands are, and without argument. Failing that, his death curse will strike you!

King Sharaeel: We are at Saher's command and service! What are his commands?

Messenger: Saher knows that Khaji has returned to your kingdom after King Khorkhis tried to kill him. He knows too that Sural has returned to the kingdom of the jinn. Sural represents a great danger.

King Asater: What do you mean by danger, messenger?

Messenger: We all know that Sural belongs to the Red Army, which is one of the strongest armies. Saher thinks that Sural can only be confronted by you and Khaji.

King Anafeer: Why can't this mission be assigned to Mared? He is stronger than both, Khaji and Sural, together.

Messenger: We don't want to waste Mared's strength on Sural. Mared is going to kill King Khorkhis.

King Zaiboun: Are we going to the battlefield too?

Messenger: Yes, you are. The kings of the jinn have gone to King Khorkhis with their armies, leaving King Aswad, King Ahmar and Sural behind because they refused to join them. You will be facing two of the fiercest kings and Sural. That's why Saher decided that you should all go to war. However, he later changed his mind and now he does not want you all to go. He wants King Sharaeel to accompany me with his army.

King Rakhel: When does Saher want us to proceed?

Messenger: Right now! There's no time. Come with me Sharaeel. Bring your army! The rest of you, prepare yourselves for the battle! Go immediately to the kingdom of the jinn and kill them all!

The kings started preparing their armies, but Sharaeel felt that something suspicious was going on. Why did Saher choose him? Why should four kings of devils face only two kings of jinn? Even if Kings Aswad, Ahmar and commander Sural were very strong, sending four kings and Khaji to face them was not necessary. Everyone left the palace to execute their orders and Sharaeel left with the messenger. The kings of the devils and their armies proceeded to the kingdom of the jinn.

King Khorkhis arrived to the kingdom of the devils. When he sent his spies to the gates, they returned and informed him that there were no guards at the gates and no soldiers inside the kingdom either.

King Khorkhis was startled with the news and thought to himself, *where did they all go? Could they be hiding and could this be a scheme to attack me?* He then ordered his spies to search further and he ordered his army to be prepared for any confrontation.

The spies returned to the king and told him that the people of the city had heard that the five kings had left two days earlier and headed for the kingdom of the jinn to fight them.

Khorkhis to his army: This means they have gone to fight Kings Aswad and Ahmar. If they left two days ago, it means they are fighting right now. Let's all proceed with our utmost speed to the kingdom of the jinn. I hope we can get there before their city is completely destroyed.

The Kingdom of the Seven Jinn

On the day that the devils arrived to the kingdom of the jinn...

One of the guards at the gates: Your majesty, King Ahmar, your majesty King Aswad, the devils are besieging the city, under the leadership of commander Khaji. They are demanding our immediate surrender!

King Ahmar: What?! The kings of the devils!

King Aswad: Are all the kings of the devils outside the gates?

Guard: Yes, all of them except King Sharaeel.

Commander Sural: So then, Khaji, you want to fight now! There is a pact between me and Khaji not to fight if we ever come face to face.

King Ahmar: Listen to me, Sural. That pact was valid when you two were close to each other. But as you can see, the situation has changed. We must stop Khaji and the four kings. If you don't kill him, he's going to kill many of our soldiers who have wives and children. Put your sentiments aside now, Sural. I assure you that Khaji would kill you when he gets the chance.

Kings Ahmar and Aswad gave their orders to their armies to fight. The war bugles sounded and everyone exchanged their ordinary insignia with the war insignia. Aswad asked Ahmar how he wanted the confrontation to take place.

King Ahmar: It is shameful to hide behind the city walls. It's either life or death. We shall go out and fight.

167

The city gates were opened. The devils were very much surprised because they thought that their opponents had surrendered. They were disappointed when they saw King Ahmar, King Aswad and Sural rushing outside with their armies, ready for the fight.

Rakhel (the devil king): Kings of the jinn, we do not want any peace pact with you! You will either surrender yourselves or your souls!

King Ahmar: You four kings of devils! You have betrayed your pact with King Khorkhis and you want bloodshed. You are well aware of the history between us and how many times we have defeated you. Go back to your kingdom before you rewrite another history of defeat!

King Zaiboun: Only weak people talk about the past! We are erasing that past and we intend to kill you all. We shall change the history of defeat to one of victory! There are only two of you here.

King Aswad: It's war then! We shall have no mercy on any of you and we shall kill you all without taking any prisoners.

Shouts for war rose and King Rakhel ordered his soldiers to throw arrows on their opponents. The jinn thwarted the arrows and launched their attack.

Fighting broke out and the kings and their commanders challenged each other. They were all very strong. It was an epic war. King Ahmar confronted King Rakhel and they struck each other with their swords and weapons. King Ahmar was severely injured in his shoulder by Rakhel's sword, but he hit back with a powerful blow on Rakhel's foot. The soldiers on both sides intervened and put an end to the fight.

King Aswad confronted King Zaiboun. Aswad was renowned for his speed and strength. He was a mixture of jinn and devils. His mother had been one of the commanders of the devils. She had been captured in one of the wars. King Aswad's father had fallen in love with her and married her. She had given birth to Aswad, who possessed the powers of both the jinn and the devils. Zaiboun could not bear the severe blows of King Aswad and his sword fell to the ground. King Aswad cut off his neck and thus, Zaiboun became the first king to be killed in that war. King Zaiboun's soldiers lowered his flag and fled to tell the other kings what had happened. Fighting raged to avenge King Zaiboun.

Khaji and Sural were in confrontation with the commanders. When they met face to face, Sural asked: "Are you going to keep your word, Khaji?"

Khaji replied: "I have to keep my promise to Saher. Pardon me, but if we don't fight each other today, we shall do it tomorrow." Sural answered him: "I'm going to keep my promise to you. I shall not confront you today." Sural moved away from Khaji and faced King Asater. It was a fierce confrontation.

Meanwhile, Khaji was fighting against King Ahmar. It was one of the harshest fights. Asater swayed under the blows of Sural's sword, and he fell down. Sural jumped over him and declared: "In your name, my God, I shall kill your enemy!" He stabbed Asater in his heart and the latter's flag fell to the ground. In the meantime, Khaji was winning the fight with King Ahmar, who had been wounded in his shoulder by Rakhel's sword. Khaji struck a powerful blow to Ahmar's wound and the latter fell down. Khaji then cut off his head. King Ahmar was the first of the seven kings of the jinn to die. His flag fell to the ground.

The jinn heard about King Ahmar's death and war became more ferocious. Of the devils, only King Rakhel and King Anafeer were left, in addition to commander

Khaji. Of the jinn, only King Aswad and commander Sural were left. Both armies retreated and fighting ceased. Each commander inspected his soldiers and casualties. Many soldiers had died in that epic battle. The devils took the bodies of their dead kings, Asater and Zaiboun, to be buried in the kings' cemetery. The jinn took the body of king Ahmar to be buried in the martyrs' cemetery. They were grief-stricken by the loss of their beloved king, Ahmar. They were all distressed by that war. They had to end it.

King Aswad: May God have mercy on your soul, King Ahmar, and may you rest in paradise. I swear by God to avenge you by killing all the devils! Do you realize what you have done, Sural? If you had confronted Khaji, this wouldn't have happened and King Ahmar would still be among us now. Your stupid promise to Khaji made us lose a great king like King Ahmar!

Sural was very sad and he wept over the loss of King Ahmar. Sural was one of King Ahmar's followers and his army was called the Red Army after King Ahmar's name which meant red in Arabic . Sural regretted not having faced Khaji and leaving his king to face him instead. He pledged to kill Khaji the following day.

The devils were furious with the outcome of the battle. Rakhel addressed his commanders: "How were they able to kill two of our kings when we were superior to them? We outnumbered them in kings and commanders! They have murdered King Asater and King Zaiboun!" Anafeer answered: "We must execute an alternative plan now. If the situation remains as such, they will exterminate us all!"

King Anafeer: Listen to me, everybody! After killing King Ahmar, only two of them represent a danger to us; King Aswad and Sural. We must come up with a plan to get rid of them. When this is done, it means we can overcome their armies.

King Rakhel: Do you have a plan in mind, Anafeer?

King Anafeer: Yes, I do. But it should be executed with extreme accuracy. It is the following: At the confrontation, you and I will go straight to King Aswad and fight him. Meanwhile, our soldiers will surround us so as to form a circle with only the three of us inside it. We fight him, protected by our soldiers who would also challenge the army of the jinn. Our army would be a fort in which we fight Aswad and kill him. The same will be done with Khaji. Our soldiers will surround him when he's fighting with Sural. This way, there will be two circles; one for us and the other for Khaji. When we kill Aswad, we throw his body outside the circle and over his soldiers who would then retreat. We kill them while they are retreating. And you, Khaji, will do the same. When you kill Sural, you throw his body outside the circle so that his soldiers will see it, surrender and flee.

King Rakhel: It's an excellent plan, Anafeer! However, I want to add one detail to it. When we confront Sural and King Aswad, one of our soldiers, at our signal, should attack them from the back.

The devils agreed on the plan and started getting ready as dawn was approaching. The soldiers set out to the battlefront. The bugles of the jinn were blown and the drums of the devils were beaten. The armies launched their attack. King Rakhel and King Anafeer headed straight toward King Aswad, while Khaji headed toward Sural. They executed their plan. King Aswad was startled by what was happening. He found himself facing two of the kings of devils and encircled by their soldiers. The army of the jinn tried to lift the siege, but it was too tight. At the same time, Khaji was blockading Sural, and the

171

confrontation began. It was too much for King Aswad who was standing up alone against two devils. He was tired out by the confrontation. The devil in charge of the attack from the back was waiting for the signal, but Rakhel thought that he would be able to kill Aswad on his own after tiring him out.

King Aswad fell to the ground following the numerous blows from the swords of Rakhel and Anafeer. His blood flowed on the ground and Kings Rakhel and Anafeer stood looking down at him while he was struggling between life and death. Anafeer said: "It's amazing how you looked yesterday, king of the jinn, and how you look today! Fighting death on your own land and looking up at the sky waiting for the angels to come and take your soul. How weak you are now!" King Aswad seemed to have died of his many severe injuries, and as King Rakhel carried him to hurl his body at his soldiers, King Aswad snatched King Rakhel's sword and cut off his head. Aswad was only faking death.

With his head cut off, King Rakhel fell down. King Anafeer was taken aback! As soon as King Aswad attacked him, the devil waiting for the signal stabbed Aswad in his heart and took it out. Anafeer was shocked by what was happening and he cut off Aswad's head shouting and cursing: "Damn you, Aswad! You still carry the devilish blood that you inherited from your mother." He threw Aswad's body outside the circle to his soldiers who fled upon seeing the corpse of their king. King Aswad's flag fell to the ground.

Meanwhile, Khaji was in a crucial confrontation with Sural. Both of them sustained severe injuries and their bloods flowed everywhere. The devil was waiting for Khaji's signal but the latter rejected the idea of treachery.

The two of them were very tired and Sural said: "By God, I shall kill you to avenge King Ahmar!" Khaji replied: "And I shall kill you for killing King Asater!" Khaji fell to the ground and Sural raised his sword saying: "Pardon me, my friend, but it's my duty now." But as Sural was about to kill Khaji, the devil attacked him from the back and cut off his head. Commander Sural died and Khaji was infuriated by what the treacherous devil had done and cried out: "Idiot, did I order you to kill him?" Khaji was very sad for the loss of Sural; he was as dear to him as a brother. He killed the treacherous devil and wept over the corpse of Sural. The siege of the devils was lifted after the murder of Sural.

When the jinn knew what had happened and that they were left without commanders or kings, they tried to escape to the city and the devils followed them. The victory belonged to the devils who were exhilarated with it. Their joy didn't last long, however, when they saw the army of demons hovering over them. King Khorkhis arrived to the battlefield with his demons. The jinn were happy to see Khorkhis. The devils were frightened at seeing the transformation of Khorkhis and they fled to King Anafeer and Khaji to tell them that Khorkhis had arrived with his army of transformed demons.

King Anafeer didn't know what to do then. He was alone with Khaji. He commanded: "Attack and kill them all, and I shall take care of Khorkhis." Khaji was afraid of Khorkhis and didn't want to face him. He knew that his own power was no match to the demons' power. So, Khaji secretly fled the battlefield along with some of his soldiers. King Khorkhis ordered the killing of all the devils, and the demons attacked them. The demons were much stronger than the devils and the latter started falling down one by one. King Khorkhis descended on the

173

battlefield and started killing the commanders of the devils until he came face to face with Anafeer. He shouted at him: "You traitor king of devils! You have betrayed me after sealing your pledge of allegiance to me! By God, I shall not forgive you; I shall kill you!"

Anafeer replied: "You have arrived very late your majesty! Kings Ahmar and Aswad and Sural are all dead." King Khorkhis didn't believe what he heard and he attacked Anafeer. Anafeer was no match for King Khorkhis and the latter cut off his head with only one strike. Anafeer's flag fell to the ground and King Khorkhis ordered his soldiers to kill all the devils and not take any prisoners. The demons killed all the devils that fought in that war. The ground was covered with blood and corpses. The place looked like a vast graveyard.

After his victory, King Khorkhis entered the land of the jinn who cheered and congratulated him on his victory. He went into the palace of the seven kings of the jinn and heard the details of the battle from one of the soldiers. He was saddened by what had taken place and he knew that all the remaining kings of the jinn will be very sad also. Khorkhis then asked the soldiers about Khaji's whereabouts and they told him that he had escaped right after his arrival. King Khorkhis then said: "So Khaji has run away from the battle! We shall meet later Khaji! You can't go very far."

Khorkhis returned to his kingdom bearing unpleasant news and carrying the dead bodies of King Aswad and Sural to bury them in his land in remembrance of their bravery

The Cursed City

King Sharaeel arrived to the Cursed City escorted by the messenger and was received in Saher's palace. Mared, Markhof and Sourfag were also in attendance. Saher welcomed King Sharaeel but he was somehow agitated. He had been waiting for news of the war from his spies. Saher's magic depended now on the result of the war. He had formulated several equations and placed two betting options. One bet was on the defeat of the jinn and the other was on the defeat of the devils. He chose the former bet. If the devils overpowered the jinn, the curse would fall on the land of the jinn and their entire population would become his prisoners to use in his magic.

Saher's spy arrived bearing the news. He announced: "Master Saher, you have won your bet with the defeat of the jinn."

Saher: If I did win, then why isn't their city cursed yet? Tell me, spy, who survived from the kings of devils?

Spy: None of them, master. They were all killed in the battlefield.

King Sharaeel: What? The devils were all killed? How did that happen?

Shocked by the news, Sharaeel was mad at Saher. He said to Saher: "Is that your plan, Saher? Using the devils in your game to get rid of the jinn?

Saher was angered by Sharaeel's words, and retaliated: "Shut up and don't overstep your limits! I know what I'm doing. I chose you because I know you are the strongest among the devils. I need you for a greater mission. You are one of the chosen now and under my control. Don't ask too many questions or else you'll meet the same fate as your brothers, the kings!"

Saher: Tell me, spy, what happened? The magic of my curse was ineffective. I want to know the reason.

Spy: Victory over the jinn was accomplished, but the war was a real disaster. Fighting was so intense that the victims' bloods splattered up to the skies. All the kings of devils and jinn were killed and only King Anafeer and commander Khaji survived. As Anafeer and Khaji were about to enter the city, King Khorkhis arrived with his army of demons. They had changed into their bodies of fury and they were extremely strong. When they attacked the devils, the latter could not hold their own against the transforming demons, and they were killed one after the other. Even King Khorkhis attacked King Anafeer and killed him with a single blow. His force was so great that when Khaji saw it, he knew he had no chance against such force. Khaji escaped with some of his soldiers. Khorkhis had no mercy on anyone; he killed all the devils.

Saher: So we have won but this is not a real victory. Damn you Khorkhis! With this act of yours, you undid the magic of my curse!

King Sharaeel: What was the magic of your curse, Saher?

Saher: Come with me, all of you, and let me explain my bet.

They all went to the secret chamber of magic. Saher tried to show them what his bet was on. He said: "When I say bet, what do you understand?"

Mared: That you are betting on something.

Markhof: I suppose the bet has two sides.

Saher: That's right! When I say bet, it means I have to choose between two things. The bet here is either on the victory of the kings of the jinn or the victory of the kings of the devils. Each person has their own way of betting. In my bet, I chose the victory of the devils because I knew there were four of them while there were only two of the jinn. The devils are stronger then. For the bet to be complete, the equation must be achieved. If the devils win, then at least one of their kings would remain alive to become responsible for the bet. Afterward, I shall place the contract in that king's body and cast my curse upon the desired area or land or person.

However, if one side of the equation falls or if one of the provisions is imbalanced, the bet becomes void. This has just happened, my friends, when Khorkhis interfered and killed King Anafeer That's why the curse failed. Khorkhis has invalidated the magic of the curse by killing the last king of the devils that was betted on. The bet was emplaced in Anafeer's body when King Aswad died. But then Anafeer was also killed and the bet died with him.

King Sharaeel: So, what should we do now that the plan has failed?

Saher: I had courted on making the city of the jinn a cursed city so that I could use its people as scapegoats to empower my magic. But what shall we do now?

Markhof: Why don't we launch an attack on Khorkhis in his kingdom and kill them all? We are mighty and strong.

King Sharaeel: They too are mighty and strong! Don't forget that Khorkhis has transformed himself and so has his army of demons.

Saher: This is strange! I had put Khorkhis under the foolishness spell. Where did he get the idea of attack? Could the magic have been undone?

Mared: Why do you suspect that? You said yourself that this kind of magic cannot be undone.

Saher: I sense something wrong. Spy, go to the palace of King Khorkhis. Hide there and keep a watch over them. Take a look at Khorkhis' body and see if Thabeel, who's in charge of the magic, is still inside it.

Spy: At your command, master.

Sourfag: I have a plan, Saher.

Saher: What is your plan?

Sourfag: If we want to defeat Khorkhis and his comrades, we should get rid of them one after the other, without letting them realize it.

Saher: What do you mean, Sourfag?

Sourfag: I mean that if we attack them in their kingdom, there's a big possibility of incurring huge losses on our side. But if we fight each one of them separately, we can win.

Saher: Yes, but how?

Sourfag: I am commander of the sea beasts. My real power lies in the sea. After the death of Sural and the escape of Khaji, Khorkhis is left with only four strong commanders:

1- Commander Darl: Commander of the princes of the Valley of Fire. Their power lies on land. They are mighty and we all know it. The Valley of Fire was once called the graveyard of the Ashkhor family.

2- Commander Shuja: Commander of the army of commandos. They are famous for blowing themselves up in the enemy's land. They do not fear anything and they are also characterized by treachery. They used to dwell in mountains and caves and such people stand out with their might.

3- Commander Fifgel: Commander of the flying jinn. Their great speed and high flying are outstanding as is their sharp eyesight. We all know they are very strong jinn.

4- Commander Torn: Leader of the sea nymphs. I hate their kind. They are my arch enemies in the seas. Their strength lies in the seas and they can compete with my strong beasts.

Now that we have sorted them out and got to know the extent of their strengths, let us not forget King Khorkhis, who is a demon. Demons are well known for their great might. They are a rare branch of jinn and they can transform themselves when in a state of war. They become taller and stronger. They can also fly and they become so strong that no one can compete with them.

Our forces are:

1- Commander Mared: Prince of the merdan who are reputed for their might and strength on land.

2- Commander Markhof: Commander of the savage ogres. They are known for their ruthlessness and willingness to destroy anything that comes in their way.

3- Commander Sourfag: Commander of the sea beasts. I stand out with my power in the sea and the ability to control its waves.

4- King Sharaeel: King of the devils who are well known for being very fast fighters.

Now I want to make something clear. We have to lure them, one after the other. I shall start the war by luring Torn to the sea and fighting him there. No one can interfere in that situation. Me and my beasts we outnumber the nymphs of commander Torn. I shall blockade him with the waves and defeat him. Torn is younger than me and he's less experienced.

Saher: Just a moment, Sourfag. I've just had a brilliant idea. You have inspired me with your plan. In the book of Mushawaz 'The Black Palace', and in the book of

Kahen 'Prediction and the Biggest Blasphemy', there was an equation that stated that if we three unified our forces, we would be able to make a whole city disappear and thus assume complete control over it. But that was just an equation which we did not put into practice as we were occupied with other issues. However, we have already established its foundations and formulas.

Mared: What do you mean by making a whole city disappear?

Saher: During that period, Kahen predicted that one of the kings was going to attack, kill and crucify us and make us a lesson and an example to others. We thought a lot about that. We didn't have an army to defend us, but we had our brains that were worth many armies. After much thinking, we came up with the idea of hiding the armies, capturing them as prisoners and dumping them in a labyrinth from which they could never get out.

King Sharaeel: Please explain more, Saher. You have lost us with your labyrinth!

Saher: Kahen had predicted that that king would be one of the flying jinn. Our idea was to join our forces and equations together to formulate the biggest and strongest equation; one that was flawless and undecipherable. We named it The Triangle of Death. These were its conditions:

To complete the equation, the three of us—Mushawaz, Kahen and Saher—had to be the executors. We were the foundations of all the magic, conjuration and prediction equations in the world. Without our equations and the equation of the beginning, no act of magic or prediction could be achieved. We had linked all the equations to us and to our names. We established schools and many pupils graduated from them. The idea of The Death Triangle came from that inspiration.

The equation of The Death Triangle was formed like this: The three of us stand in a pyramid shape. Mushawaz is at the top of the pyramid, with Kahen and me below it. Then we make the equations of magic, conjuration and prediction.

Mushawaz, at the head of the pyramid, equals Saher, the first foot of the pyramid and equals Kahen, the second foot of the pyramid. These three are equivalent to the equations of disappearance which are similar to the riddles of Habel and Nabel. Therefore, Mushawaz's power supports the head, Saher's power supports the right foot and Kahen's power supports the left foot. Thus the powers of the three foundations are joined together and they form all the equations of magic, conjuration, prediction and riddles. These lead to the cavity of ruin, i.e. that which swallows anyone who passes over it or enters in it. This is the same as getting lost in the labyrinths of magic, conjuration and prediction. Getting lost equals the power of every act of magic, conjuration and prediction. Therefore, the power of the triangle increases with every act of the above and thus these acts would nourish the triangle. That would be the biggest contract in the history of the foundations, stamped by the foundations' own blood. It would last until an unspecified day. The equation ends with Kahen as the second foot of the pyramid, and Saher as the first foot of the pyramid and Mushawaz as the head of the pyramid. As you see, the equation began with Mushawaz and ended with him. This means that it's an infinite circle, which also means that it can never be unraveled. It becomes more efficient with time. Any act of magic, conjuration or prediction that is done anywhere in the world, only strengthens the triangle and nourishes it. Just imagine how many acts of these kinds are carried on worldwide! This is an extraordinary triangle that will make anyone who goes inside it disappear.

Mared: How can you complete this equation, Saher, when you're the sole foundation now? Mushawaz is on Khorkhis' side, and Kahen was murdered by you!

Saher: Even if Kahen died, his body still lives. In that body lie the power and ability of Kahen which we can extract. As for Mushawaz, I'm going to abduct him.

Markhof: How are you going to bring Kahen's body when it's buried in the Valley of Worship? Do you want us to pull it out of his grave?!

Sourfag: Kahen's tomb is in the highest mountain in the Valley of Worship. We can dispatch one of our flying soldiers to bring his body to us.

Later on, the spy that Saher had sent to check the reason for the failure of Khorkhis' magic spell arrived. He said, "Master, I have bad news."

Saher: What is it, spy?

Spy: Master, Khorkhis' magic spell had been undone. I didn't find Thabeel or any of those who were in charge of the magic.

Saher: What? How did that happen?

Spy: Mushawaz made it happen, master.

Saher: Damn you, Mushawaz! You are still as smart as before! Distancing yourself from this science hasn't affected you. This means that I shall have to challenge you again, my mentor, but this time I shall get rid of you!

Spy: Master, there's something else.

Saher: What is it?

Spy: Father Sumia is on their side now.

Silence prevailed. Everyone looked scared. Father Sumia's alliance with King Khorkhis and his interference in this war meant that they were going to lose it. They all feared Father Sumia because they knew that he was the most powerful of the jinn and their first father. They were all his descendants and they respected and feared his wrath. Besides, they knew that Father Sumia never fought, but his interference and alliance with Khorkhis meant that he was going to fight, if need be. That was something they did not desire.

Mared: My God! If Sumia is now involved in the war, we'll never be able to w n it!

King Sharaeel: And now, Saher, what do we do?

Saher: We must form The Triangle of Death. It's the only solution.

Saher began assigning missions to each of them with great caution. They were going to face the greatest power. He delegated King Sharaeel to go with one of the flying devils to the highest mountain in the Valley of Worship in order to bring Kahen's body to him. Mared, Markhof and Sourfag were charged with preparing the armies for the war. Saher took it upon himself to abduct Mushawaz. He proclaimed: "You must execute my orders very carefully. The failure of any one of you means death to all of us. Repeat after me: 'Fire to my assistants and peace to my enemies'. You will thus be stronger with my curse."

They all departed; each one to accomplish his mission. King Sharaeel flew on the wings of the fast bird of devils to the Valley of Worship. Saher left to execute the abduction of Mushawaz. Mared and his comrades set about preparing their army for the impending war.

The Valley of Worship
(The Abduction of Kahen's body)

King Sharaeel arrived to the Valley of Worship. He headed towards the foot of the mountain where he perceived Kahen's grave. He felt scared. Kahen was entombed in a very impressive shrine. He entered the shrine and started digging out the grave. It was a rainy day and the sound of thunder reverberated between the mountains of the Valley of Worship. When he finished digging, he brought out Kahen's tomb, but when he opened it, he didn't find Kahen's body. He was startled by the appearance of Habel and Nabel.

King Sharaeel: What's going on? Why did you come here?

Habel and Nabel: We have been ordered to kill you.

King Sharaeel: How dare you do that! Woe unto you traitors when Saher knows about your evil intentions!

Habel and Nabel: King, get ready to die!

King Sharaeel took his sword and aimed it at Habel and Nabel. He then heard the voice of Saher saying to him: "Calm down, King! What's taken over you? Why do you want to kill Habel and Nabel?"

King Sharaeel: Saher! Aren't you supposed to be abducting Mushawaz? Why did you come here too? Do you want to kill me? Why? I was the first one to support you and your war. I didn't protest to the murder of my brothers, the kings of devils. I agreed to everything you did. Now you are repaying my kindness and loyalty by killing me! Why?

Saher: Do you remember when I told you that I needed you for a bigger assignment? That assignment was killing you, you devil king! I'll tell you why. You must know before you die because your time in this life is up.

King Sharaeel: You mean the plan that Sourfag was talking about was just a ruse?

Saher: Indeed. We had prepared the plan before you came to us. But we talked about a plan so that you wouldn't suspect us.

King Sharaeel made an effort to fight, but his body stopped moving. Saher paralyzed him by reading some charms over his body. King Sharaeel was shocked by his inability to move and shouted, "What have you done to me, traitor!"

Saher: I am not a traitor. It is you who have betrayed your brothers! And now I shall tell you why I chose you. Ever since my war against Mushawaz and Kahen, I have lost all the servants and sentinels of magic. I have been preparing a new army of magicians since then. The idea of the Triangle of Death was a strong and ingenious one but how could I implement it after Mushawaz's repentance and Kahen's death? I thought a lot and formed many equations and many people were killed as sacrifice to the Triangle. However, it was useless because the three original foundations had to be present to stamp it with their blood and make it complete. Even when I formed the equation of exchanging the foundations and exchanged Mushawaz and Kahen with Habel and Nabel, the equation of the Triangle of Death didn't work out. It should have been stamped by the blood of the original foundations and not the new ones. Not only that, the three foundations should have belonged to the same branch of jinn and possessed the same magical star. Magical stars are like fingerprints;

they don't match. Centuries later and after thorough prediction, Habel and Nabel found out that you and Mushawaz came from the same branch of jinn and that both of you had the same blood and magical star. This is something that very rarely happens. In the world of magic, you possess Mushawaz's blood and characteristics.

And now, with Kahen's body in my possession, I shall again switch the equations of exchanging the foundations and return everything to the way it was before. I shall remove Habel and Nabel for the time being and then bring them back after completing the equation of The Triangle of Death. That's why I have to kill you now and take your blood and that of Kahen's to stamp the equation of The Triangle of Death. Do you understand now why I chose you? Why I told you that I needed you for a bigger mission? Don't be sad, King of Devils, I'm going to call it The Diabolic Triangle, in recognition of you and all the other kings of the devils.

After that, Saher started returning the equations of the foundations to their original form. At the time of his war with Mushawaz, he had used Habel and Nabel so that the magic, conjuration and prediction would not end. Now he was going to restore the original equation in order to make the new Diabolic Triangle work. Habel and Nabel made a drawing of the equation and it was applied accordingly. He placed King Sharaeel on top of the pyramid, instead of Mushawaz, and Kahen's body at the left foot of the pyramid, while he placed himself at the right foot. Saher brought back the three foundations to their positions and began to chant and read magical charms. A strong wind started blowing over the Valley of Worship and heavy rains poured. The Valley of Worship was situated near the sea, and the power of the magic brought down the land in which The Diabolic Triangle was placed below the sea level. Waves surged over the city of the Valley of Worship and drowned it in the sea. After finishing with the exchange equation, Habel and Nabel cut off the heads of King Sharaeel and Kahen, took some of their blood and stamped the equation of The Diabolic Triangle with it. Saher also stamped it with his blood. Following this act, the city was completely submerged in the sea and it disappeared. The people of the city tried to escape but it was useless. The triangle encircled them and imprisoned them inside it. The only one who was able to escape was a flying jinni who happened to be outside the triangle. He flew to Father Sumia, who was still in the kingdom of Khorkhis, to inform him of what had happened.

When Saher was through with the equation of The Diabolic Triangle, he placed his curse in it to make it last forever. He undid the curse of the Cursed City and placed it in The Diabolic Triangle, where he also put every curse and equation of magic, conjuration and prediction that their books contained. Having done that, Saher found out that the triangle had more power than he expected. King Sharaeel and Kahen were fixed inside it so there was no need to return Habel and Nabel to the equation as foundations. The equation of the three foundations was protected in the triangle. He linked that triangle to the universe and it became the strongest magic equation in the whole world. He then linked it to all the sins committed in the world, whether they were murder, adultery or sodomy among others. Whenever any one of the jinn committed a sin, the triangle became more powerful. He also created a city from that triangle and named it The City of Taboos. People of that city had to kill each other and commit as many sins as they wished in order to give more power to the triangle. The Valley of Worship was transformed into the Valley of Taboos and after that, The Diabolic Triangle became the most powerful magical act in the ancient world as well as in our contemporary world.

Finally, Saher ordered Habel and Nabel to summon Mared and his comrades and to move him to his new location—The Diabolic Triangle.

The Kingdom of Khorkhis

The kingdom of Khorkhis grieved over the death of King Ahmar, King Aswad and commander Sural. The jinn were very sad over their loss and outraged at the devils' betrayal. But what was the use! They had lost two of their greatest kings and the devils had lost all their kings as well. To honor them, King Khorkhis ordered the burial of King Aswad and Sural in the Royal Cemetery of Martyrs and he had a statue erected in the kingdom in recognition of their glory. Father Sumia took the kings aside and addressed them: "We must unite now and face Saher to prevent him from wreaking havoc in the country." At that moment, the flying jinni arrived. He was severely wounded and close to death.

His ghastly appearance shocked everyone there. Father Sumia asked what was wrong with him and he replied: "Saher has killed all the people of the Valley of Worship!"

Sumia: What? He killed all the people? What about the soldiers? Where were they at the time?

The flying jinn: Saher took us by surprise. He performed a very powerful act of magic at Kahen's shrine. The city sank to the bottom of the sea. The strange thing was that anyone who tried to escape disappeared, and anyone who tried to fly over the city disappeared too!

Sumia: How were you able to escape?

The flying jinn: I wasn't inside the city at the time but not far either. I started feeling very weak as soon as I approached the city. I don't know what happened to me! In fact, I feel like I'm dying right now!

189

Mushawaz: My God! What are you saying? You mean that everyone who had passed over the city disappeared?

The flying jinni: Yes, they have, and I don't know where they went! The whole city disappeared into the bottom of the sea. Anyone who tried to leave it was not seen anymore. It was an awful sight!

Mushawaz: My God! Saher has done it! But that's impossible.

Sumia: What's wrong, Mushawaz? What has Saher done?

Mushawaz: This is the equation of The Death Triangle. But how was he able to execute it without the blood of the two foundations, myself and Kahen? How did he do it?

Sumia: What is this triangle?

Mushawaz: We thought of that triangle at the time when we were performing our evil acts. Kahen had predicted that one of the kings of the jinn would attack us and kill us. As we had no army to challenge him, the idea of the triangle came to us. That triangle conceals anyone who passes over it or through it. But it was too strong an idea, because if we executed the equation, the ground where the triangle was installed would cave in. Thus we thought of applying it on a sea-side city, so that the city would sink below sea level and drown into the sea. As a result, anyone who passed over the city would disappear and become trapped in it. It would serve as a prison and the captured people would serve as sacrifice in our acts. The only flaw in the triangle was the time element. Its effect had a limited time. So then we thought of linking it to our acts, evil acts and sins, to provide it with strength. Later on, we thought, we would link it to the world of the jinn and every vice committed would give the triangle more power. The more sins were committed, the stronger the triangle would become. There would be anarchy, crimes, adultery ... The inhabitants of the city had to commit sins to be able to leave it. However, we wouldn't let them leave the city; we would just make them believe it. We would encourage them to disobey God as much as possible. They would commit the biggest blasphemies so we would allow them to get out. But what they didn't know was that the body of anyone whom we helped to get out would be used as sacrifice in our acts of magic, conjuration and prediction. His body would be fit for sacrifice because his blood was saturated with blasphemy and vice. That equation, though, couldn't be completed without being stamped by the blood of the three of us. So how did Saher succeed in completing it?

Sumia: Oh God! Do you mean that the people of the Valley of Worship are all prisoners in the city, and that they must disobey God to be able to get out of it?

Mushawaz: Unfortunately, yes. This triangle is flawless. No one can disable its effect!

Khorkhis: So, what should we do now?

The flying jinni: Father Sumia, hasn't the time come yet to kill Saher?

Sumia: By God, it is time! Get up, all of you, kings and commanders, and get ready for war! I shall lead you myself this time.

Sumia then went outside the palace of King Khorkhis. He held the bugle of unity. That bugle had a story in the world of jinn. It was connected to all the branches of the jinn; devils, demons, merdan, ogres and beasts among others. When Father Sumia sounded that bugle, all those who heard it had to get ready to fight under his leadership. The bugle had an extremely loud and powerful sound that could be heard by all the branches of jinn everywhere. Whoever didn't comply with the rules would be killed.

Father Sumia sounded the bugle ten times, and then he announced: "Now, all the jinn population will go to war against Saher." Mushawaz then dressed Sumia in the green colored war costume. He wore his green armor and a headband on which was written 'I testify that there's no God but Allah'. He ordered all the kings and commanders to wear headbands with the words 'there's no God but Allah'.

Khorkhis set about preparing his army of demons and ordered the other kings and commanders to do the same. They all left the palace with Father Sumia in command. Khorkhis was standing on his right side and Mushawaz was standing on his left side. The kings and commanders all took their positions behind the king.

That army was truly the strongest army in the whole era of the jinn. Afterwards, all those who had heard the bugle of Father Sumia came and gathered outside the palace. It was an awesome sight. The entire jinn population was getting ready for war with the exception of the women and children.

Father Sumia declared in front of the gathering crowds: "One of my offspring has become a tyrant and I condemn him to death!

His name is Saher and he is accompanied by Mared, Markhof, Sourfag, Habel and Nabel. They also have some of the jinn branches on their side. They have legalized crime, murdered innocent people and shed the blood of women and children. I swear to God, I shall have no mercy on them! And not only that, Saher has drowned my own city and imprisoned its whole population. They are now under his command. By God, there will be no mercy on him and his supporters. I want you all to stand in one line and repeat after me: Determination, determination, until we reach the summit!"

The army of jinn shouted Father Sumia's words. They repeated that phrase until the ground shook under their feet!

The armies then moved, led by Father Sumia, King Khorkhis, Mushawaz, kings Saleh and Katel, queens Tuyour, Houran, Sheikha, and commanders Fifgel, Torn, Shuja and Darl.

No one was left behind in the kingdom of Khorkhis or in the cities of the jinn and devils. Everyone went to fight under the banner of Father Sumia. They all headed to the Valley of Worship.

King Khorkhis: Father Sumia, how shall we penetrate the triangle now?

Sumia: I don't know, but perhaps Mushawaz does.

Mushawaz: Father, if you want me to face Saher, then I'll have to challenge him with my conjuration.

Sumia: But you have repented, Mushawaz! In the past, while you were at the peak of your power, you couldn't overcome Saher. How will you be able to do so now after having abandoned these acts for such a long time? Also, Saher has become much stronger than before.

Chamberlain Bilban: Master Mushawaz, you have undone the magic spell of King Khorkhis by reciting God's name over him. Why don't you do the same with Saher?

Mushawaz: You're right, Bilban. Mentioning God's name is more powerful than Saher's magic and sorcery. I shall use God's name against Saher.

Queen Tuyour: How do you want us to launch the attack, Father Sumia?

Sumia: We shall see. Be patient. There's a time for everything.

193

The Diabolic Triangle

Saher stood looking at his triangle, feeling very proud of his achievement. He started celebrating with Mared and his comrades, Habel and Nabel, and the rest of the servants and sentinels of magic. That triangle was a dream of his. It was the most powerful act of magic in history. He told his friends: "I shall conquer the world with this triangle and place everyone under my command!" One of Saher's priests came running to him and informed him that an army that consisted of all the branches of jinn, under the leadership of Father Sumia, was heading towards them at that very moment.

Saher: Who are the commanders of this army?

Priest: Father Sumia is at the head of this army with King Khorkhis, Mushawaz, the kings of the jinn and the four commanders.

Mared: At last, you have come, Khorkhis! I'm going to kill you myself.

Saher: Don't underestimate them, Mared. Don't forget that they are led by Father Sumia. Your power is no match to his. He's the father of the jinn and the strongest among them. They will go to the Cursed City thinking that we are still there.

Markhof: So what shall we do?

Sourfag: Can The Diabolic Triangle make them all disappear, Saher?

Saher: Yes it can, provided that we force them to pass over it. But how can we do that when there are so many

194

of them? If one of them disappears, the rest will find out. Remember that Mushawaz is with them and he knows the secret of this triangle and that the city that drowned is Father Sumia's city. Sumia will be suspicious when he doesn't find his city.

Habel and Nabel: Master, we have bad news!

Saher: What is the bad news at this difficult time?

Habel and Nabel: We've heard from our spies in the kingdom of Khorkhis that Sumia already knows about the disappearance of the Valley of Worship, and that Mushawaz knows the secret of its disappearance and that it was caused by The Triangle of Death.

Saher: And how can he know all that? Could he have predicted it or perhaps he has his own spies among us?

Habel and Nabel: Neither this nor that! One of the flying jinn was around when we cast the curse. He flew to Khorkhis and told them everything.

Saher: So Mushawaz knows now that I have completed the equation of The Triangle of Death. I must come up with a new plan. Mushawaz will be extremely cautious.

Habel and Nabel: Why don't we perform the riddles of the labyrinth?

Saher: What are these riddles?

Habel and Nabel: When they approach, we make the equation of the labyrinth riddles and cast the magic spell of disorientation on them. We support our magic with the riddles. They would flounder, not knowing where they were going. Thus, they would lose their way inside the triangle and disappear.

Saher: But the problem is Mushawaz. He is with them and he would undo the magic of the labyrinth as soon as he enters it.

Habel and Nabel: We'll cast a spell on him too and he would also lose his way.

195

Saher: How can you cast a spell on Mushawaz? This is contrary to the equation of the beginning which states that no magic or conjuration can ever touch one of the three foundations!

Habel and Nabel: Have you forgotten, master, that King Sharaeel is now the new foundation in place of Mushawaz?

Saher: That's true! Why didn't I think of that! King Sharaeel is now in Mushawaz's place, which means that Mushawaz is no longer a foundation and I can put a spell on him.

Habel and Nabel: What are you waiting for, master? Their arrival is imminent. We must cast a magic spell on the entire army, including Father Sumia.

Saher started putting together the equations of disorientation. He prepared magic charms in the names of all the kings and commanders and their armies. Then he set about killing all the population of the Valley of Worship as a sacrifice to his work. He had to kill them all. A lot of blood had to be sacrificed for that huge magic work of his which targeted kings and armies. . Mared and his comrades entered the city and began killing all the people in the name of Saher's magic. Blood colored the triangle red and corpses floated over the sea. Saher announced: "Today I'm going to defeat all those who challenged me. I own this land and I rule it with my magic. I shall curse and kill anyone who dares to challenge me!"

After finishing with the magic of the riddles, Saher told Mared about his plan: "They will be affected by the magic as soon as they enter our area. After that, they will be disoriented and lost. We shall cast a spell on their minds and eyes and make them blurry; they won't know where they are going until they end up at The Diabolic Triangle and disappear. However, this process is time-consuming and I fear that Mushawaz would realize that we put a spell on him and he would undo it. That's why I want to speed it up. I shall use you as bait. You will face them, pretending that you have been defeated, and then flee. They will go after you until you lure them inside The Diabolic Triangle where they will disappear. You must do exactly as I'm telling you to do. Forget your pride and don't try to fight them because you're no match to them. They are large in number and Father Sumia is on their side. As for the magic of riddles, I have added something new to it; it's called the Candles of The End.

Mared: What are the Candles of The End?

Saher: I placed twelve candles here, each one in the name of one of the leaders.

1. King Khorkhis
2. Mushawaz
3. Father Sumia
4. Commander Fifgel
5. Commander Shuja
6. Commander Darl
7. Commander Torn
8. King Saleh
9. King Katel
10. Queen Houran
11. Queen Tuyour
12. Queen Sheikha

I positioned each candle in the direction of the person's star. The candle will light when the person enters my land.

Markhof: But what's the use of these candles?

Saher: Each candle is connected to the person's heart. If it is extinguished, it means that that person has died.

Sourfag: Who's going to kill him?

Saher: The hidden jinn who are in charge of this magic.

Mared: Why don't you kill them without the candles?

Saher: I can't. I'm restricted by the laws of magic. Don't ask too many questions! Now go with your armies! They will be here any minute. Be prepared and execute the plan exactly as I told you. Any mistake will get us into deep trouble.

Mared and his comrades left The Diabolic Triangle and headed to the battlefield. They waited there for the enemy. Moments later, the army of Khorkhis and Sumia arrived.

Father Sumia, King Khorkhis, and the other kings and commanders arrived but they felt a strange dizziness. Father Sumia marched towards the Valley of Worship but, strangely enough, he couldn't locate its place. He was disoriented and didn't know where to go.

Sumia: My God, what happened to me? Is it possible that I don't know where my city is? Mushawaz, are we under some magic spell?

Mushawaz: I don't think so. I haven't felt any magic because Saher cannot put a spell on me. But it seems that he has done some changes to the place to get us lost.

King Khorkhis: My God, I feel weak! Could there be a curse in this place?

Mushawaz: Even if there was, how come I don't feel it?

Sumia: Let's go, kings and commanders! I know the place. It's impossible for me to get lost here!

Father Sumia was surprised by his disorientation. He tried to find his way by the landmarks that existed before, but it was useless. They marched on, not knowing where they were going, until they realized that they were back where they had started. Mushawaz tried to sense the presence of a magic charm or curse but to no avail. He suspected that Saher had put a spell on him, but deep down he knew that it was impossible. He was a foundation and foundations could never be affected by any magic.

They walked on but it was no use. No matter how long they walked, they always returned to the same place. It was like turning round in a vicious circle. Even Fifgel, the flying jinni, was lost up in the air and didn't know his way around. All of a sudden, Mared and his comrades appeared.

Sumia: Look, Khorkhis. It's Mared!

Khorkhis: You're right. He's coming our way. Come on, soldiers, get ready! Mared and his comrades are heading our way.

Mared arrived to the land of disorientation. He asked them mockingly: "How did you find your way around?"

Sumia replied: "You will know after we cut off your head, Mared! No peace to you and no mercy!

Mared: Who told you, Father, that I need your mercy? You need my mercy right now! Be prepared! I swear to God that I shall have no pity on any of you, not even on you, father!

Mared sounded the war bugles and shouted out loud: "Fire to my assistants and peace to my enemies." Father Sumia sounded his bugle and shouted: "Determination, determination, until we reach the summit!" That phrase signaled the start of the impending war between the two parties. The strongest of the forces of the jinn, Saher's army and Sumia's army, were going to challenge each other. That was the most ruthless war in the history of the jinn. Father Sumia never raised his sword, but when he did, woe to the one who dared to challenge him!

Mared stood at the front of the army with Markhof and Sourfag at his side. Behind them stood the commanders and the army of the King of Devils, Sharaeel, which was now under Mared's command. Facing them was the army of Father Sumia, King Khorkhis and Mushawaz, with the kings and commanders behind them.

The area was cursed by Saher. The weather was overcast and a strong wind was blowing. Mared launched his first assault by throwing off his poisoned arrows at them. The arrows fell like thunderbolts, but Mared's opponents resisted them. Commander Fifgel flew with his soldiers and made a violent attack on Mared, after which the army of Father Sumia advanced in Mared's direction and swords interlocked. A fierce fight took place.

Both sides were considerably strong. King Khorkhis was transformed into the invincible war demon, and Father Sumia's blows struck his enemies like thunderbolts. Mared was the famous quick-and-clever combatant who could kill anyone in sight. In that battle, Markhof faced Katel, king of the jinn, and fighting intensified between them. Markhof was known for his strong build and Katel was known for his speed. The combat was fierce. Whenever King Katel aimed a blow at Markhof, the latter reciprocated with another deadly blow. The two of them started bleeding, but Markhof proved to be the stronger of the two. He cut off King Katel's head. King Katel was the first king to die in that war and his flag fell to the ground. Sumia saw what happened to Katel and hurried to his side. Markhof escaped from Sumia's sword.

In the meantime, Saher was watching the battle through his candles. After the death of King Katel, Katel's candle was extinguished. Saher knew then that Katel had died. He had actually placed the candles in that manner so he could kill each king and commander at an appointed time.

Queen Houran and Queen Sheikha confronted the devils of King Sharaeel. However, it wasn't a fair fight. The devils were treacherous by nature. Whenever Houran fought with one of them, another would stab her from the back and she would fall down. Then Queen Sheikha would come to protect Houran by killing the devil that had stabbed her. The confrontation was very tough. Commander Shuja interfered to help Queens Houran and Sheikha. He was one of the commandos and his soldiers were also known for their treachery. He asked the two queens to back off and let him handle the devils.

Father Sumia and King Khorkhis were ruthless and their might was unrivaled. Whenever they confronted their opponents, the latter would flee. Father Sumia spotted Markhof. He headed towards him and threatened: "You will not escape this time, you cowardly ogre!"

Markhof directed his blows at Father Sumia but the latter defied them. Sumia got hold of Markhof and shouted, "No mercy today!" He stabbed Markhof in his heart and took it out. Markhof's flag fell to the ground. When Mared heard about it, he became furious and went after Father Sumia to kill him. Khorkhis was waiting for Mared. He shouted: "What's wrong with you, Mared? Are you frightened now?" Mared retaliated: "By God, I'm not frightened, but I'm going to avenge Markhof's death by killing you!" He struck a very powerful blow on Khorkhis' shoulder that injured the king's arm. Khorkhis struck back at Mared and an indescribable battle ensued. Khorkhis stabbed Mared's foot and Mared fell to the ground. As Khorkhis was directing the final blow at Mared, the latter took him by surprise and stabbed him in the abdomen. Khorkhis fell down. Mared held his sword and threatened the king: "Today, I shall put an end to your life, King Khorkhis!" As Mared raised his sword, commander Darl came to the king's rescue and cut off Mared's hand with his sword.

Sourfag was in confrontation with commander Torn. It was a battle between the sea beasts and the sea nymphs. Saher sensed the danger because Mared had not followed the set plan. He ordered the hidden jinn to tell Mared to withdraw to The Diabolic Triangle. When Mared was informed, he complied. His soldiers withdrew and fled. Father Sumia's army followed them, while Fifgel, Torn and Shuja flew in the pursuit of the devils, followed by the other kings. Father Sumia and Mushawaz suspected that something was wrong. Mared's army reached The Diabolic Triangle, which Saher had hidden by putting an illusionary city in place of the sea to lure Sumia's army into it. Sumia's army fell in Saher's trap. As soon as they entered that city, Saher read the talisman of The Diabolic Triangle, and the real triangle appeared. Water flooded the whole place and one by one the soldiers disappeared.

Mushawaz, Sumia and Khorkhis were shocked by that frightful sight. Armies were disappearing before their very eyes. Commanders Fifgel, Torn, Shuja and King Saleh all disappeared with their soldiers. It was unbelievable. They all froze in their places not knowing what to do. The triangle had swallowed more than half the army and their numbers were diminished considerably. They were startled and speechless. Saher came out and said: "Fire to my assistants and peace to my enemies."

Mushawaz: How did you do that, Saher? How could you do it without my blood? I'm one of the foundations!

Saher: Welcome, my master! It's been a long time since we last met. You've become an old man.

Mushawaz: How did you do it Saher? How could you complete the equation of the triangle without my blood?

Saher: What's the use in telling you now! Your time is running out!

Mushawaz: Running out? What do you mean?

Saher brought out the remaining candles and put them in front of Mushawaz. Mushawaz realized that they were the conjuration candles that he had written about in his book 'The Black Palace'. He asked, "How did you dare do that, Saher?" And Saher retorted: "I haven't done anything! It's your own equation, the Equation of The Candles."

Sumia: What are these candles, Mushawaz? Why are our names on them?

Mushawaz: These candles were my idea. They are linked to our hearts at the moment. I see now the hidden jinn directing their swords at our hearts. As soon as a candle goes off, the jinni in charge of the magic would kill the one whose name is on that candle.

Sumia: You mean that if Saher extinguishes the candles now, we all die.

Mushawaz: Yes, but he cannot extinguish them all at the same time. Each candle will go off by itself when the appointed time comes. This is the strongest of my equations. I wrote it in my book but I didn't know that Saher was familiar with it. It's strange that he put my name also on a candle, which means that he was able to cast a spell on me too. That's why we lost our way. I didn't feel the presence of any magic because I was bewitched, just like you.

Khorkhis: What's the solution, Mushawaz?

Mushawaz: There's no solution now. I shall confront magic with conjuration one more time. I pray to God that I can overcome Saher.

Saher: What do you intend to do, Mushawaz? I've become stronger than you. Do you really want a confrontation?

Mushawaz started reciting the old conjuration chants. He intended to disable the effect of the candles. Saher used his reverse equations. He used the mirror equation against Mushawaz. He was following Mushawaz's own method to overpower him. But this time, Mushawaz stopped the chanting and began to recite the praises of God which had a much stronger power than Saher's magic. Saher was surprised by that; he could not understand what was happening. How could Mushawaz recite conjuration chants and then the praises of God! The praises of God were undoing Saher's magic. He got scared and felt pain in his body. Habel and Nabel sensed the danger and tried to put barriers between the praises of God and Saher. Then Saher decided to break the appointed time and extinguish the candles one by one before Mushawaz could disable their effect. He put out the candles of commander Darl and Queen Sheikha. The two of them felt pain in their chests and fell to the ground. Blood started spilling out of their mouths and they died from Saher's magic. Habel and Nabel created very strong winds and a big storm to keep Mushawaz away from Saher. Thus, they were able to escape from the battlefield and enter The Diabolic Triangle.

This time, Saher was defeated by the mention of God's praises and not by Mushawaz's conjuration. However, the losses were enormous. All the Kings of the Jinn had died except Khorkhis and Houran. Sumia and Mushawaz also survived. Dead bodies were scattered everywhere. That was the biggest loss for the jinn because most of their population participated in that war. Their numbers on Earth diminished because of these wars. As soon as they retreated from the battlefield, they encountered Khaji with some of his soldiers. He implored: "Please forgive me, I want to fight on your side against Saher." Sumia replied: "We have lost many lives and we no longer have an army to face Mared and his comrades. Most of our kings and commanders were killed." All of a sudden, Mared, Sourfag and their soldiers launched a fierce attack on them from the back. Sumia's soldiers were affected by the cursed place and their bodies weakened. They had to confront Mared or else be killed, so they started to fight back. Suddenly, Khaji attacked Sumia; he had tricked them! He aimed his blows at Sumia's body, which made him shout angrily, "Were you bluffing us, idiot?" Sumia struck a fatal blow at Khaji's neck causing him to bleed to death in slow suffering. Mared was fighting King Khorkhis with one hand— because his other hand was cut off by Darl—and Khorkhis proved to be the stronger of the two. As Mared fell down bleeding, Khorkhis aimed a fatal blow at his heart but missed it. Sourfag then attacked Khorkhis from the back and stabbed him in his heart. Khorkhis fell dying to the ground and when the demons saw him, they attacked Sourfag and cut him to pieces, much aggrieved and angered by what had happened to their king.

Mared, who was severely wounded, retreated with his soldiers following him. Sumia commanded: "Let them go, don't follow them! This might be another plot." The demons surrounded King Khorkhis. He was bleeding, fighting death. When Sumia went to him, Khorkhis said: "I have betrayed the pledge of the Ashkhor Dynasty. I wasn't the king that my father, Khafan, wanted me to be."

Sumia: By God Khorkhis! You were greater than your father. History will remember you and I shall inscribe your name on the pages of the jinn dynasty.

Khorkhis: What will you write, Sumia? A king who failed to defend his land or King Khorkhis was the last king of the jinn?

Sumia: I shall put down in writing that you were the last and greatest king of the jinn.

Khorkhis: I swear I can see the sky opening its gates!

Sumia: Don't be afraid! God is with you. Don't forget that you have His name inscribed on your forehead. Repeat the name of God and if He wills, heaven will be your abode.

Khorkhis: I testify that there is no God but Allah, the Creator.

Those were King Khorkhis' last words. Khorkhis—king of the jinn and devils, and the last king of the Ashkhor Dynasty—passed away. Everyone cried; the demons, the jinn, the devils and the soldiers. Even Father Sumia sobbed and embraced him in his arms. The demons carried Sumia and flew him to Khorkhis' native land. The armies followed them. When they reached the kingdom, the people thought that Khorkhis' army had returned victorious. But when they saw the body of King Khorkhis held by Father Sumia, they all started crying. It was a day of grief and sorrow. The whole city shed tears over the king. Sumia entered the king's palace where Fouta was waiting for him. Fouta collapsed when he saw Khorkhis' dead body. He couldn't believe that the king had died. Khorkhis was so young and he was the last of the Ashkhor Dynasty.

Sadness prevailed in the kingdom. Father Sumia announced: "We must bury him now, Bilban. He's a martyr." The palace servants proceeded with the funeral arrangements, disbelieving their king's death and fearing Saher's power at the same time. Saher had defeated all the kings and commanders. The demons roamed the kingdom, escorting the king's body to his burial place near his father, King Khafan.

Mushawaz: What shall we do now, Sumia?

Sumia: I shall sound the bugle of unity to find out who's left of the jinn branches.

Sumia did just that, but no one came. Many jinn had died, and the few who survived, had run away to escape the war.

Thabeel: Master Mushawaz, haven't you noticed something?

Mushawaz: What is it, Thabeel?

Thabeel: Do you remember when we undid the magic spell of King Khorkhis? You said that it was strange that the spell remained even after the nymph who was one of the bases of Khorkhis' magic spell, was killed. I told you then that Saher had put a replacement in one of the bodies.

Mushawaz: I do remember that. And if all the bases die, the person in whose body is the replacement, would die too!

Thabeel: Master, when you challenged Saher, didn't you notice something?

Mushawaz: What's that, Thabeel?

Thabeel: The replacement appeared in Saher. He had put the replacement in his own body.

Mushawaz: Is that possible? Was Saher that crazy as to put the replacement in his own body? My God, what have you done to yourself, Saher! This means that after the death of all the persons mentioned in his contract, he would die too!

Thabeel: That's right, master. Queen Houran, you are the only survivor. If you die, Saher would die too because he would have lost his bet.

Queen Houran: If my death should put an end to that defiled man's life, then I'm ready to die!

Sumia: Stop talking like that, Houran! We don't need any more losses. We need you now. Thabeel, you told me that the jinni in charge of Houran had entered the wrong body. He entered the body of her maid-in-waiting. Houran killed her and Houran's base thus fell.

Thabeel: I did say that. But when Saher put the replacement in him, everything went back to what it was before.

Queen Houran: Father, don't forget that if Saher doesn't die, he's going to destroy the world. Don't forget also that our kings and commanders are captives in his triangle. Saher would sacrifice them and gain more power.

Silence pervaded the king's chamber. After careful thinking, Mushawaz proclaimed: "I swear by God that it's going to be hard on us to kill you, Houran!" Houran replied: "I only want to do that to save our kings and commanders who are imprisoned in Saher's triangle. It's me in return for all the kings. I'm ready to sacrifice my blood for their sake. Pray to God to grant me martyrdom."

Sumia was silent for a while then he said: "It's very hard for me to do that. But if this is your wish, Houran, then you'll be a martyr in God's eyes." Are you certain, Mushawaz, that if we kill Houran, Saher would die too?"

Mushawaz: Yes, this is the replacement and we were the ones who formed this equation. When all those who were bewitched die before the magic is executed, the holder of the replacement that was betted on, dies too.

Sumia: Queen Houran, are you sure of your decision?

Houran: Yes, I am. I shall sacrifice my blood to make the accursed Saher die. We are all in God's hands.

Houran requested to die according to the laws of the kings of the jinn. Those laws stated that the condemned kings should stand upright by themselves and be stabbed in their hearts to bleed to death. Her request was granted. The execution rituals were carried out and Houran requested the judge to come to her. The judge asked her: "Queen Houran, do you know what you're doing?" and she answered, "Yes." The judge of the jinn held his book and wrote the name of Houran, the martyr, in it. He grabbed the sword of justice. Houran asked him to inscribe her name near the name of her nymph whom she had killed unjustly. The judge did as she told him and wrote Houran's name on the sword near that of her nymph.

The judge then ordered the war costume to be taken off Houran and to dress her in the costume of the kings of the jinn with a crown on her head. Houran stood up with her head toward the sky, reciting the testimony before dying and asking God to accept her martyrdom. The judge raised the sword of justice and stabbed Houran in her heart. Houran's pure blood flowed while the judge's eyes welled up with tears. Queen Houran, the last queen of the jinn, died. Sumia said: "May God have mercy on you, martyr queen. We shall never forget your sacrifice. After Saher's death, peace will rule the earth."

Thabeel laughed maliciously. He said: "You fools! You fell in the trap! The replacement is not inside Saher's body. It's inside your body, Mushawaz. Saher put it there during the last confrontation between the two of you."

Everybody was shocked by Thabeel's words. Mushawaz felt that he was dying and he fell down. Thabeel fled to tell Saher what happened. The soldiers tried to follow him but he had disappeared from sight. Mushawaz was fighting death. He felt stabs and strong blows on his chest. He saw what was happening to him. The servants of magic had attacked him and were stabbing him everywhere to make him suffer before dying. Sumia was helpless. Mushawaz's blood was flowing everywhere and his body was being cut up. The jinn were hidden and Sumia and his people couldn't do anything. Mushawaz told Sumia that the hidden servants of magic were killing him. He said: "Father Sumia, you are the only hope left now." Mushawaz drew his last breath. His body was all cut up and his injuries were severe. Sumia, the sole survivor, stood alone after all the kings had been murdered. He raised his hands to the sky imploring God to forgive him and have mercy on him and on all the vulnerable people.

Chamberlain Bilban: Master Sumia, what shall we do now?

Sumia: I swear to God I don't know! We can only pray, Bilban. Leave me alone now. I want to pray.

The soldiers, Bilban, and Fouta left the room, scared and shocked. Their defeat was imminent. There was no one but Father Sumia after the death of all the kings and commanders. They began to pray. Prayer was their only salvation.

Sumia went out to the palace garden, reflecting on the dark unknown future. Bilban and Wise Fouta approached and told him: "Master Sumia, there isn't any king of jinn and devils anymore. You are the only one who can hold this position. What do you say, master? We need a leader!"

Fouta: Master, you should assume the position of king right now. Please reconsider!

Sumia: I hate this position! You know Fouta that I've never wanted to rule. Ruling is a burden and I'll be responsible in front of God for all my subjects. It's a heavy load, Bilban.

Bilban: But master, what else can we do? Without a leader, there will be chaos. The whole population wants no other king but you.

Sumia: Let me think about it, Bilban. I want to be alone now.

Bilban: As you wish, master. Please give this matter some serious thought. There's no other ruler but you and if you refuse this position, anarchy will prevail in our country.

Bilban and Wise Fouta departed, leaving Sumia with his thoughts. Sumia continued praying and asking for God's guidance till dawn.

Sumia heard strange voices and the sounds of bugles that were different from those of the jinn's. The sound was coming from the sky. Sumia looked up and saw one of the angels coming towards him. He felt very scared. The angel descended and greeted him: "Peace and God's mercy and blessings upon you." Sumia answered, "And peace upon you too." The angel said: "Do not be afraid, good servant of God. I am the angel Sarafeel. God is furious with the jinn and he ordered us to kill all the evil-doers. They have greatly disobeyed God and although He has given them time to repent, matters have become much worse."

Those words scared Sumia! God's fury was frightening. He said: "Heaven forbid God's fury! What is my mission, angel Sarafeel?

Sarafeel: Take all the good and weak people in addition to the women and children out of this city. Take them down to the valley at the foot of this mountain. That land

211

will become a holy land and it will be named Mecca. Take whoever you deem good and righteous. We shall invade your land. It's God's will.

Sumia: I have faith in my God. Whatever He wills, he does. I shall do what you asked me to do, but what about us?

Sarafeel: Have no fear, good servant of God. There is a time for everything. I'll give you three days to take whomever you wish to Mecca. We shall not harm anyone who goes to that land.

Sumia's heart beat quickly and he perspired profusely. He returned in a hurry to the palace of King Khorkhis and shouted at the top of his voice: "Where is Wise Fouta? Where is Wise Fouta?" Fouta hurried to him: "What's wrong Father? What is happening?"

Sumia: Do you remember Khorkhis' dream, Fouta?

Fouta: Yes, I do. What about it?

Sumia: An angel called Sarafeel came to me and told me that God was furious with the jinn. The angels were going to roam the country to rid it of the evil-doers.

Fouta: Father, is what you say true? When did that happen?

Sumia: Just a while ago. Come with me and take a look at Sarafeel's footprint. It has left a hole in the ground.

Sumia and Fouta went out to the garden where Fouta saw the imprint of Sarafeel's foot. Fouta was very scared. He asked Sumia: "What did he tell you, Sumia? Are we going to die too?"

Sumia: No. He instructed me to take all the righteous people and the women and children to a valley below this mountain called Mecca. He said that peace would be upon anyone who entered Mecca. He granted me three days to accomplish this task before the angels launched their war against the jinn.

Fouta: Then, father, what are you waiting for? Let's gather as many people as we can and head for Mecca.

Father Sumia, Fouta and Bilban started gathering as many people as they could. Some people believed Sumia but others didn't. They had lost their faith in him. Many said that they were going to stay with Saher to be safe from his curse. Sumia tried to convince them but it was futile. The situation was chaotic. Murder, theft, rape and kidnapping were rampant. With no one to lead them, the army was dispersed. Sumia took whoever agreed to go with him and left the kingdom. When the people saw that, they thought that Sumia had escaped. The situation deteriorated. Those who remained wanted Saher to be their ruler. Father Sumia sounded his bugle one last time but to no avail. He went to the kingdom of jinn and devils to calm them and explain what was happening but they mocked him and told him that he was afraid of Saher. The world of the jinn was turned upside down. There were no kings to rule them and no armies to deter them. Everyone wanted to be a ruler. They were all fighting with each other. Sumia and the few people who accompanied him went to Mecca. Sumia said to Fouta and Bilban: "My God! What has happened to the jinn?"

Fouta: By God, master, even if you became their ruler, you couldn't have controlled them. Evil and greed fill their hearts.

Sumia: Let's take refuge in Mecca now. The fate of our own world is unknown. What Khorkhis had seen wasn't a dream, it was a vision! What was the end of the dream, Fouta?

Fouta: Khorkhis said that the angel told him that God was going to send others to rule Earth, other than the jinn dynasty. That's what I don't understand yet. But everything will become clear eventually.

Sumia and his people arrived to Mecca and hid themselves there. They started reciting the name of God to avoid his anger. They all feared the wrath of God. Sumia told them: "You should thank God for being merciful to you."

The Triangle of Death

After mentioning God's name over his body, Saher began to feel intense pain. But he was able to heal himself with his magic. Saher said to Habel and Nabel: "Get ready to sacrifice all the people in the city of The Triangle of Death. I must increase my power. Where is Mared?"

Habel and Nabel: Master, Mared is suffering from a serious wound near his heart. It was caused by King Khorkhis.

Saher: And how is he now?

Habel and Nabel: We don't know, master. We have left him in the care of doctors.

Saher's spies later arrived and informed him that Sumia and his companions had fled to an unknown place after the people in the kingdoms of jinn and devils revolted against him. They told Saher that the people were cheering and calling out his name and that they wanted Saher to be their leader because they didn't trust Sumia anymore.

Saher: That's wonderful news! Very soon, I shall be ruling the world and I shall be the first magician ever to be in that position. Go now, Habel and Nabel and kill as many as you can of the prisoners in my Diabolic Triangle. Sacrifice them in my name to give my magic more strength and power.

Habel and Nabel: At your command, master.

Habel and Nabel started killing the prisoners in The Diabolic Triangle, one after the other. With each sacrifice, Saher's power increased. They killed the kings

and commanders and Saher reached the peak of his power. Not knowing what fate had in store for him, Saher shouted repeatedly, "Who can challenge me?"
Saher asked one of the foretellers: "Predict for me! Am I not going to be the greatest king on Earth?" As soon as the foreteller began his prediction, he fell down and died! Saher, Habel and Nabel were startled and they wondered what had happened to him. Every time someone was asked to predict for Saher, he would fall and die. Saher said: "What's happening to them? Is it possible that Mushawaz had put a spell on them to kill them?" Then Thabeel came to Saher and told him: "I made them kill Queen Houran and Mushawaz also died." Saher replied: "But if Mushawaz died, how can his magic equations kill the foretellers? Something weird is going on! I shall find out later but now, let's go to the palace of the Ashkhor Royal Family. I shall take over the kingship and become the king of the jinn and devils."

The Last Reign

On the morning of the third day, Saher headed to the kingdom of King Khorkhis with his retinue, guards, servants and soldiers. Mared, having recovered, accompanied them. When they reached the gates of the kingdom, winds blew strongly and they heard very loud sounds. Saher asked: "What is this? What's going on? What is that sound? It's different from the sound of the jinn's bugles!'" Habel and Nabel said: "It's probably one of Sumia's plots against us."

Thabeel: But Sumia has fled. Could he have tricked us?

What they didn't know was that the angels were going to fight them. That sound was coming from the bugle of angel Sarafeel, who was leading the army of the angels, consisting of six hundred angels only. The sunlight was blocked. Saher looked upward and was surprised to see the angels above them. He called out loud, "It's the angels!"

Upon seeing the angels, Saher's entourage was terrified. Sarafeel sounded his bugle one more time and the ground beneath their feet shook and crackled. All the jinn heard the sound of the bugle and were frightened. Sarafeel sounded his bugle again and again until an earthquake struck. Landmarks changed, volcanoes erupted, the ground was flooded and the earth cracked and swallowed many of the jinn population. The army lines of Saher were dispersed. As the soldiers tried to flee, the angels attacked them and killed them. Even Saher ran away because he knew that his magic had no

217

effect on the angels. The angels followed the jinn and started killing them.

The angels roamed the earth, exactly like Khorkhis had seen in his dream, and entered the kingdoms of the jinn and devils and killed all the traitors there. The jinn escaped to the mountains, seas, forests, caves and valleys. The angels captured some of Saher's assistants to give them a fair trial. Angel Sarafeel searched for Saher and found him hiding in a cave with one of the devil boys. Sarafeel addressed Saher: "Look what you have done to yourself, Saher. You have been unjust to yourself and to those who supported you. You created a curse for yourself and defied God. And now, God's curse is cast upon you, you accursed magician!"

Saher: I beg you not to kill me! I shall repent and ask for God's forgiveness. I'll never do that again.

Sarafeel: It's too late, Saher! God has been patient with you, but you have gone way beyond the limits. You murdered people and sacrificed them in your name. You rebelled against God and continued with your evil work until you formed The Diabolic Triangle which encouraged all kinds of vice. How unjust you have been to yourself!

Saher: I asked you to give me a chance, angel. I'll return to my senses.

Sarafeel: It's too late, Saher! Be prepared to die and meet God. He gave you a reprieve until you got what you wanted. Then you shouted: "Who can challenge me? Who can challenge me?" Here I am challenging you, Saher! What are you going to do now?"

With his pure hand, Sarafeel grabbed Saher's neck and lifted him up. Saher started reading a talisman in an attempt to bewitch Sarafeel. Sarafeel smiled and said: "Are you trying to bewitch me, Saher? I, angel Sarafeel, the good servant of God, am immune to your magic. We

218

have killed all the jinn that you used in your magic acts and no one is left." Sarafeel took his sword and said: "In the name of God always! This is the end." He cut off Saher's head, held it and said, "**Accomplished with the grace of God.**" Then he blew the victory sound which signaled the execution of his mission. Some angel soldiers went to him and told him that they hadn't found Mared, Thabeel, Habel and Nabel yet. He said: "Leave them to me. They are hiding in a forest and I shall go to them now." Then he stopped talking and looked at the little devil boy. He asked him, "What's your name, boy?" And the boy answered, "My name is Izraeel." (The wicked Lucifer).

Sarafeel: Where are your parents?

The boy: I don't know!

Sarafeel to his soldiers: Take him to heaven as a prisoner. If he's left here on his own, he will die!

The angels took Lucifer along with the other prisoners to heaven. King Sarafeel carried on with his mission. He headed to where Mared, Thabeel, Habel and Nabel were hiding. He caught them unawares. He said, "Eternal peace or total destruction." They answered: "Fire to my assistants and peace to my enemies." Sarafeel said: "My God, what is this? Are you cursing me, you defiled people? Your Saher is dead and he's now up in the sky in God's hands. You want to cast Saher's curse on me? God's curse is on you now!"

Habel and Nabel: What are you going to do to us, angel? Do you want to kill us? We beg you not to. Saher bewitched us all to make us his servants.

Sarafeel: No, he didn't! You are evil and bad yourselves. If you had repented like Kahen and Mushawaz, you would have been victorious. But you treated your people unjustly and you abandoned your faith.

219

Thabeel: I only did what I did because I had to feed my children. I needed money.

Sarafeel: God provides for every child in this world. Killing people is not an excuse to feed your children. You, Thabeel, betrayed Mushawaz and killed him intentionally although you had the chance to repent. But you have a vicious heart, so do not ask for forgiveness today because God's curse is upon you all.

Mared: I was betrayed by King Khafan and he sent me into exile to the Forbidden City for no reason. Later, his son Khorkhis wanted to kill me. How could I not defend myself, angel?

Sarafeel: Patience is a virtue, Mared. Even if Khafan and Khorkhis treated you wrongly, you had no right to kill innocent people and support Saher by sacrificing them in his name. What Khafan and Khorkhis did to you does not give you the right to disobey God!

They were all speechless. Angel Sarafeel declared: "Today I shall rid the world of your evil and accomplish the mission assigned to me." He drew his sword and said, "Accomplished with the grace of God!" And he cut off their heads, one after the other.

Having executed his mission, Sarafeel exchanged the insignia 'There's no God but Allah' with another one 'Accomplished with the Grace of God'. He sounded his bugle to announce the greatest victory and the execution of the mission. The angels gathered around him and told him that they had imprisoned and killed all those who had been loyal to Saher. They also told him that some of the jinn escaped or hid in caves, valleys, mountains, forests and seas. Sarafeel asked: "How many of the jinn population are left?" One of the angels replied: "Only a few. Do you want us to kill them all?" Sarafeel said: "No. God's mercy has saved those who are left." Come, angels, let's go back to heaven. Our mission here on Earth is finished. I shall follow you after I speak to the good servant of God, Sumia.

Angel Sarafeel went to where Sumia was staying and entered wearing his white attire. On his forehead, the words 'Accomplished by the Grace of God' were written. He greeted Sumia: "May peace and God's blessings and mercy be upon you."

Sumia: And peace upon you, angel Sarafeel. Tell me what happened.

Sarafeel: We have relieved the world from the evil of Saher and his assistants. I killed Saher, Habel and Nabel, Mared, Thabeel and all those who helped them.

Sumia: Thank God for this victory! They had become so evil and vicious that I wasn't able to deter them anymore.

Sarafeel: Good servant of God, we have killed so many of the jinn and imprisoned many of them as well. Of your descendants, only a few thousand are left and they are hiding in caves, valleys, mountains, forests and seas.

Sumia: What are your orders, angel? What do you want me to do now?

Sarafeel: God has responded to your prayers. He was merciful to you. But you will no longer be the masters of Earth.

Sumia: What do you mean, angel?

Sarafeel: The jinn must stay out of sight. They will inhabit the caves, valleys, mountains, forests and seas that they escaped to. This is God's will, good servant of God!

Sumia: God has willed it and I am His obedient servant.

King Sarafeel: I bid you farewell, good servant of God. I hope your children will learn from their mistakes and return to their senses.

Sumia: I only ask for God's forgiveness. My children tyrannized Earth and God's judgment was fair.

Sarafeel ascended to the sky and all the jinn disappeared. They were no longer masters of Earth. They tried to coexist and adapt themselves to their new conditions. They were divided into sects and kingdoms and tried to keep away from evil. They feared God's wrath.

They all repented and asked for God's forgiveness. Sumia gathered them and said: "You see my children what has happened to us because of Saher's greed and tyranny? We must learn our lesson and never again resort to disobedience or tyranny."

The jinn population started leading normal lives and mating so as not to become extinct. But in spite of that, evil exists in the world no matter how hard we try to eradicate it. With the passing of time, some jinn collected the books of Saher, Mushawaz, Kahen, Habel and Nabel in an effort to follow in their example but they failed. Just like the jinn tried to regain some of their former glory, Saher's pupils tried to restore the glory of their mentor. But all their efforts were futile. They didn't know how to formulate contracts or equations. The books of the three foundations were very complicated and during the war with the angels, all the teachers of magic, conjuration and prediction had been killed. They could only make riddles and amulets which were incomparable to contracts, as they had a very weak effect.

In that period of time, Lucifer was a young boy living in heaven. The angels loved him and they raised him as one of their own until he grew up and became a good servant of God. The pampered boy was very popular. He worshipped God more than anyone else did. But when God created Adam, Lucifer was very jealous of him and did not worship him. By doing that he disobeyed God. He persuaded Adam and his wife Eve to eat from the forbidden tree. God was furious with the three of them and he sent them to Earth. They had become His enemies. Lucifer asked God to grant him a respite until Judgment Day and said that he was going to take all the descendants of Adam and Eve to hellfire with him. God granted Lucifer a respite. Lucifer had defied God.

When Lucifer descended to Earth, it had undergone some changes after Sarafeel's war with the jinn. Sumia and the jinn heard about the incident between Lucifer and God. They realized that Lucifer had defied God but that God had given him a respite and was not going to make him die until Judgment Day. They found out too that God had sent to Earth a ruler other than the jinn and that ruler was Adam and Eve (peace upon them) and their posterity. Sumia understood then the meaning of Khorkhis' dream.

Lucifer embarked on forming an army of jinn and devils and anyone who wanted to join him of the branches of jinn. He set up his throne in The Diabolic Triangle, which is known today as the Bermuda Triangle.

Adam was getting accustomed to life on Earth, after living in heaven, and started to create his posterity. He also defied the accursed Satan.

Hence, the New Era began, the era of the sons of Adam and the sons of Lucifer. That war has not ended yet. It's been an ongoing war until our present day.

God put a partition between us and the jinn. We have become the masters of Earth while the jinn inhabited valleys, seas, forests and caves. At the start of the New Era, Satan could not influence the sons of Adam except by temptation. Later, after reading the books of Saher, Kahen and Mushawaz, and learning their acts, Lucifer realized that he could penetrate the partition by implementing magic equations and laws. That was the only solution. He was able to do it and to teach some of Adam's sons the science of magic, conjuration and prediction to use in their lives and bewitch each other and cause disorder just like Saher and his companions had done. The conjurors and magicians of Adam's posterity were ranked according to the capabilities of each one of them. Most of them used riddles, which are considered weak magic.

Rarely did anyone execute any act of magic through a contract. To reach that level, one had to worship Lucifer and deny the existence of Allah. Lucifer passed the books of magic, conjuration and prediction over to the descendants of Adam and thus gave rise to discord among them. Lucifer's ongoing war against Adam and his progeny had started since the day God created him. He has his own army and kingdom, children and ministers. They all live at present in The Diabolic Triangle (the Bermuda Triangle).

In ancient times, there were the good servants of God who challenged Saher and his assistants, like King Khorkhis, the kings of the jinn, the four commanders, Mushawaz, Kahen and Father Sumia. God has also appointed some of his good servants to challenge Lucifer and his assistants. There were three of them supported by armies of righteous individuals. However, I am in no position to disclose their identities. Their names are mentioned in the Holy Koran. They work and fight while in hiding. This is one of the secrets of the universe which I am at no liberty to reveal. However, I did let you in on one of the secrets of the universe, hoping that you would benefit from it. Perhaps we can all learn from their mistakes and not repeat them. We seek refuge with Allah from the accursed Satan.

- The End -

(We are no longer masters of Earth. The children of
Sumia must coexist with the children of Adam.)
The Royal Chamberlain, the Wise Shansibal
15/4/1745 A.D.

(Today, I witnessed the greatest challenge since The Last
Reign: An Arab family bewitched by a magic spell much
more powerful than that of the Ashkhor Royal Family. All
sorts of magic and conjuration arts had been used in that
spell. They were written in the original contracts. This is
considered the first ever act of magic carried out in the
style of Saher and Mushawaz billions of years after their
death. Not one of the sheikhs of the sons of Adam was
able to solve the mystery of that family's magic or undo
it. The family members almost died. But God sent three
of his good servants with their soldiers to assist them. It
wasn't any more a question of undoing the magic; it
turned into a fierce challenge, with the family as victim.
The magic was sealed by a worm from Lucifer's horn.
Another great history wrote about the war between that
family and the good servants of God and their soldiers
against the magicians of the sons of Adam and Lucifer, in
addition to their followers and servants of magic and
conjuration. That war has not ended yet and it is still
going on until our present day. It started in the year 1980
A.D. and heightened in the year 1999. A.D. Let us all pray
to God to end this new war)

Prince of the Sea, the Ogre Sulbian
1/12/1999 A.D.

INDEX